wisdom from

the five people
you meet in heaven

wisdom from

the five people
you meet in heaven

Brandon Gilvin
Heather Godsey

CHALICE
PRESS

ST. LOUIS, MISSOURI

Cover art: FotoSearch
Cover and interior design: Elizabeth Wright

This book is printed on acid-free, recycled paper.

Visit Chalice Press on the World Wide Web at
www.chalicepress.com

10 9 8 7 6 5 4 3 2 1   04 05 06 07 08 09

Library of Congress Cataloging–in–Publication Data

Gilvin, Brandon.
  Wisdom from the five people you meet in heaven / Brandon Gilvin and Heather Godsey.
      p. cm.
  Includes bibliographical references and index.
  ISBN 0-8272-3025-7 (pbk. : alk. paper)
  1. Albom, Mitch, 1958- Five people you meet in heaven. 2. Religion in literature. 3. Heaven in literature. I. Godsey, Heather. II. Title.
  PS3601.L335F5934 2005
  813'.54—dc22

                                                2004025389

Printed in the United States of America

For Jane McAvoy,
a Scholar, Mentor, and Friend,
whose vision made books like this one possible

contents

introduction

Everyone has an idea of heaven, as do most religions, and they should all be respected. The version represented here is only a guess, a wish, in some ways, that my uncle, and others like him—people who felt unimportant here on earth—realize, finally, how much they mattered and how they were loved.

—From the Dedication page of
The Five People You Meet in Heaven

Writing a novel about heaven seems like an ambitious venture. Heaven—life after death—eternity—such concepts are staggering because they push the limits of our creative abilities. It's a difficult enough task for a writer to use her imagination to bring to life a historical period such as Elizabethan England or to render a fictional representation of

1

Abraham Lincoln in a way that not only preserves historical accuracy but also expresses a sense of Lincoln's humanity. But heaven? How can we imagine a place (if it really can be called a place) that no one can describe, outside of those who claim to have had mystical encounters or "near-death experiences"? It seems to be an impossible task. No wonder the countless theological tracts, misguided scientific experiments, and sensationalist television documentaries that have attempted to answer the question of what heaven might be like leave us a little unsatisfied.

But something about Mitch Albom's *The Five People You Meet in Heaven* makes it different from overly sentimental movies and hyper-empirical scholarship. Not only is Albom's book a good read, but it seems to be about more than just what happens to us after we die and "make it past the pearly gates," so to speak. Rather than just describing Albom's vision of heaven, the book *seems to tell us something about the lives we are leading right now.*

This should not be surprising. Our culture is awash with insights—reliant on popular psychology and popular sociology—about what our imaginings about heaven might reveal about who we are, what our deepest desires are as individuals, or what we as a society value above all else. But even as we look at the Christian tradition, stories about heaven, the afterlife, and the apocalypse tell us about so much more than their direct subjects. According to the gospel of Matthew, Jesus began many parables with the phrase "The Kingdom of heaven is like...." Since its early days, the church has used these parables to teach about not only what it might be like to experience heaven but also how the ethical and spiritual character of Christian community should be shaped.

As we discussed *The Five People*, it became clear that its pages present more than a beautiful vision of heaven. We can also glean some important insights into the lives we lead in the here and now. But how should we discuss that sort of insight? After some deliberation and discussion, we came to a conclusion—we could begin the conversation by discussing the wisdom tradition of the Hebrew Bible. The wisdom tradition of the Hebrew Bible comprises a number of books, including Proverbs, Ecclesiastes (also called Qoheleth), Song of Solomon (also called Song of Songs), and Job. Some of the psalms also are noted for displaying wisdom characteristics.

Wisdom literature such as Proverbs, Qoheleth, and Song of Songs are generally attributed to Solomon, the Israelite king celebrated for his wisdom. But most textual and archeological evidence points to dating wisdom books later than the Israelite exile, which ended in 538 B.C.E., whereas Solomon reigned from 961–922 B.C.E.

The actual authors of these books are unknown, but are generally associated with teachers (Qoheleth) or the elite social class known as sages (Proverbs). Wisdom literature finds many parallels in the wisdom traditions from other ancient Near Eastern cultures. Job, for example, resembles early Egyptian, Sumerian, and Babylonian texts, whereas the sayings from Proverbs find parallels in Egyptian and Mesopotamian literature.[1]

Wisdom literature encompasses styles as variant as collections of teachings and admonitions, poetry, and didactic dialogues between humans and the divine. Likewise, its theology is unique to the Hebrew Canon. Rather than emphasizing themes such as covenant, law, or ritual, wisdom literature offers practical instruction on the ways to live a happy life and maintain an orderly society, and on ways to achieve wisdom, as well as philosophical rumination on existential crises. In other words, wisdom writing expresses an interest in the way individuals experience life. Richard J. Clifford notes common features of the wisdom books:

---

[1]Ancient Near Eastern texts are readily available in James B. Pritchard, ed., *Ancient Near Eastern Texts Relating to the Old Testament*, 2d ed. (Princeton: Princeton Univ. Press, 1955), 405–54; William W. Hallo and K. Lawson Younger, Jr., eds., *The Context of Scripture*, vol 1: *Canonical Compositions from the Biblical World* (Leiden: Brill, 1997), 110–36, 213–30, 359–66, 483–98, 540–44, 561–94; W. G. Lambert, *Babylonian Wisdom Literature* (Oxford: Clarendon Press, 1960).

1. Few of the books…say anything about the history of Israel, its major institutions of covenant and kingship, and its great personalities, such as Abraham and Sarah, Moses, and David.
2. The name of Israel's God, Yahweh, does not even occur in Qoheleth and the Job dialogs (Job 3—37).
3. "Righteousness in the books is not linked to observance of the law and covenant or to performance of rituals as it is elsewhere in the Bible.
4. Genres and themes of neighboring literatures are far more obvious in the wisdom books than in other sections of the Bible.
5. The books all share a strong didactic tone.
6. The word "wisdom" pervades all the books…There is persistent attention to wisdom in itself, which makes these biblical books different from their canonical counterparts.
7. These books are, of course, concerned with practical wisdom—knowing how to live well, how to perform one's tasks, and how to understand the secrets of the universe. But the Bible goes beyond specific instances of wisdom to explore the nature of wisdom, its importance and limits, and its relationship to Yahweh.[2]

Because of its combination of concerns for practical wisdom and the philosophical nature of wisdom, we have chosen wisdom literature as the backdrop for our discussion. This is especially apropos since, as Albom seems to suggest in his dedication to his uncle, *The Five People You Meet in Heaven* may lead us toward a discussion about what is truly important in life.

We have focused this discussion by paralleling each of the characters Eddie meets in heaven with the themes and insights from a particular selection from wisdom literature. The first chapter, focusing on the plight of the Blue Man—the first person Eddie meets—will look at Ecclesiastes/Qoleleth and

---

[2]Richard J. Clifford, "Introduction to Wisdom Literature," in *The New Interpreter's Bible*, vol. 5 (Nashville: Abingdon Press, 1997).

the fairness of life. The second chapter will focus on the Captain and the nature and necessity of sacrifice. The third chapter examines the relationship between Eddie and his long-estranged father in the context of the issue of forgiveness as presented by the wisdom psalms. Chapter 4 will tie together the biblical love poem known as The Song of Songs and the great love of Eddie's life, Marguerite. In chapter 5 we will tackle the question of suffering, as the fifth person Eddie meets is the young girl Tala. We will tie this chapter to the consummate wisdom text on suffering: Job. Our book will conclude with a discussion of wisdom literature, its orientation toward life, and how that affects our understanding of Eddie as a character.

The chapters are brief and include suggested books for further reading as well as questions to spark discussions. As we explore the life of Eddie, the lives of the people he meets in heaven, and the biblical texts that add insight into Albom's work, we hope that you will begin to imagine not only what this might mean for your vision of heaven but also what it means for the life you lead now and the wisdom you glean from it.

Albom's title lures you into expecting new insights into the nature of heaven. You may approach the book asking what you can expect to experience during the expanse you vision as eternity. You may want a description of the "mansions" that await you there. Perhaps you are curious concerning the nature of God's throne or the types of rewards you receive for eternity.

If these are your questions, Albom's book will disappoint you. Albom gives us no new information or theory about the long-term experience of heaven. He simply lays out a prelude to heaven, what one learns on the final leg of the journey before settling down for eternity. For Albom the central concern lies not with the nature of heaven. It lies with answering ultimate questions as to why we live and what we live for. Albom wants to show that "each affects the other and the other affects the next, and the world is full of stories, but the stories are all one" (196).

Interestingly, the wisdom books of the Bible take the same approach. These biblical books may represent the divine voice in divinely inspired scripture, but they say little about the divine abode. They concentrate on earthly matters from a heavenly perspective. Ultimately they seek to describe the life that "fears the LORD." Thus Proverbs begins by stating that "The fear of the LORD is the beginning of knowledge" (1:7). It concludes by announcing that "Charm is deceitful, and beauty is vain, but a woman who fears the LORD is to be praised" (31:30).

One might conclude that Albom fears ignorance, not knowing the consequences of life's actions and decisions, whereas scripture fears the LORD as the only source of knowledge. Both perspectives give us food for thought. Placing them side by side challenges us to ponder the source(s?) of true wisdom.

CHAPTER ONE

the blue man and the teacher

The Blue Man held out his hand. "Fairness," he said, "does not govern life and death. If it did, no good person would ever die young."

(*FIVE PEOPLE*, 48)

Just as you do not know how the breath comes to the bones in the mother's womb, so you do not know the work of God, who makes everything.

(ECCL. 11:5)

You have to feel a great deal of sympathy for Eddie. Arriving in heaven would have to be a confusing thing. You can share his expectations and imagine his disappointments. At first glance heaven does not appear to meet any of his expectations.

Then, of course, the first person he meets is a man the color of a "graying blueberry," sitting alone in a chair on a stage. This is Blue Man, the sideshow freak. Eddie shakes his head violently, screaming NO! Reading his thoughts, the Blue Man voices Eddie's thoughts, "'No? It can't be heaven?' he said. 'Why? Because this is where you grew up?'" (34). No, this can't be heaven. Especially when it looks a lot like Ruby Pier, the old amusement park that was such a large part of Eddie's life and one of the strongest sources of his ambivalence about the meaning and importance of his life.

Again Blue Man has an answer: "Well. People often belittle the place where they were born. But heaven can be found in the most unlikely corners. And heaven itself has many steps" (34). But for Eddie, "the thought that this was some kind of blessed resting place was beyond his imagination."

The Blue Man persists: "People think of heaven as a paradise garden, a place where they can float on clouds and laze in rivers and mountains. But scenery without solace is meaningless" (35).

The Blue Man's job, it seems, is to welcome Eddie into heaven and to impart to him the first of five important lessons.

Moreover, the lesson from the Blue Man does not provide Eddie with the information he most desperately wants—did the little girl who was sitting beneath Freddy's Free Fall live? Instead, the Blue Man shows Eddie that as a boy, Eddie was responsible for a chain of events that killed the carnival performer. Eddie is shocked and devastated. In turn he wants to know if he will be punished for what he believes is his sin. As the Blue Man has already explained, these revelations are not part of a punishment that God heaps upon those who die. Instead,

> "This is the greatest gift God can give you: to understand what happened in your life. To have it explained. It is the peace you have been searching for."
> (*Five People,* 35)

But what does the Blue Man explain to Eddie about what happened in his life? How could anything come out of an explanation about his culpability in the death of another human being but guilt or judgment? How does such a senseless act ever make sense?

We will certainly explore the answer the Blue Man provides. To do that, we should first establish a context for how we understand what he says, and for that we turn to the Book of Ecclesiastes, or *Qoheleth.*

10

Ecclesiastes: The Teacher

The title *Ecclesiastes* comes from the ancient Greek translation of the Hebrew title of this book, *Qoheleth*. *Qoheleth* means "Teacher" and refers to the narrator to whom the sayings and teachings in the book are attributed. As is the case with so much of the wisdom literature, tradition and an inscription in the first verse of chapter 1 attribute its authorship to Solomon. Most scholars believe it was written far too late to evidence Solomon's actual influence on the text, generally dating it in the fourth or third centuries B.C.E. W. Sibley Towner concludes that "The language of Ecclesiastes demands that it be placed among the later books of the Hebrew canon...The book exhibits the 'philosophical' spirit of the Hellenistic period to a degree more pronounced than any other book of the Hebrew canon, even though none of the Teacher's ideas can be directly linked to Greek originals."[1]

The most casual reader of the Bible often notes that Ecclesiastes is a little different from most of the books of the Hebrew Bible. Even in terms of wisdom literature, which diverges quite a bit from much of the typical style and theology of the Hebrew Bible, Ecclesiastes appears to be an odd book. It does not seem to follow a logical argument and often offers contradictory statements about the ways of the world. For example, Ecclesiastes begins with the Teacher's admonition that "All is vanity" (1:2) and includes sections that proclaim that wisdom, success, and hard work are all futile because all people eventually die and are forgotten no matter what they contribute to the world (1:12—2:23). However, this section ends with an

---

[1]W. Sibley Towner, "Ecclesiastes," in *New Interpreter's Bible,* vol. 5 (Nashville: Abingdon Press, 1997). But Roland Murphy, *Ecclesiastes,* Word Biblical Commentary, vol. 23A (Dallas: Word Books, 1992) sees no compelling reasons for dating outside some "Hellenistic coloring" (p. xxii). Duane A. Garrett, *Proverbs, Ecclesiastes, Song of Solomon,* The New American Commentary, vol. 14 (Nashville: Broadman Press, 1993), 254–67, ties Ecclesiastes to Ancient Near Eastern literature rather than to Greek and argues that Solomon's day is the one in Israel where such literature would be most easily accessible.

admonition promising that by living to please God, one will receive wisdom, knowledge, and joy (2:26).

Towner argues that all literature, even laundry lists, have a plot, a logical movement. Then he concedes that Ecclesiastes has an "extremely minimal" plot with "no story line."[2]

Such contradictory messages raise plenty of questions about the point of Ecclesiastes. Many nineteenth- and twentieth-century critics contended that these contradictions were the result of a gradual editorial process in which the often shocking points made by the author of Ecclesiastes were softened, redirected, or contradicted by later writers seeking to give the book a more orthodox slant.[3] Other more recent critics have suggested that the conflict within the text is not the result of a clumsy process of reining in a rebellious writer. Rather, the biblical writer intentionally points out the absurdity of life by presenting a set of conflicting extremes.

Regardless of which of the many hypotheses on Ecclesiastes's authorship seems most believable, the fact remains that it is a troubling book. Life is full of toil that is pointless. Death and war and hate are as natural a part of the seasons of life as love, peace, and birth. The hope that one finds in the prophetic texts is absent from Ecclesiastes. Likewise, the sense of social order that permeates much of the wisdom literature (as we will soon see) is absent from Ecclesiastes. Instead, what we encounter is an image of a world that is, in spite of being under the direction of God, a whirling dervish of disorder. But what lies behind such a perspective on life? Roland Murphy, pointing to 9:10, argues that "Qoheleth loved life… It was because of his appreciation of life and wisdom that he perceived the awfulness of death and the vanity of life itself."[4] Building on this, Towner sees Qoheleth's weight coming down

---

[2]Towner, 276.
[3]Murphy, xxxv–xli, surveys various opinions.
[4]Ibid., lxix.

"on the opportunity for human happiness in a world in which God is utterly sovereign and people are truly free."[5]

But what relevance does such a view of life have for the lesson of the Blue Man? Let's take a look.

The Balance of It All

As a child chasing a baseball, Eddie set off a series of events that ultimately led to a wreck that triggered a heart attack for the weak-nerved Blue Man. When the Blue Man reveals this, Eddie assumes that he will incur divine wrath, punishment, or retribution for his actions. Instead the Blue Man reveals that he has something to teach Eddie:

> "That there are no random acts. That we are all connected. That you can no more separate one life from another than you can separate a breeze from the wind." (*Five People*, 48)

The Blue Man goes on to explain that this interconnectedness intricately ties the life of one human being to the death of another. Although we may look for a sense of fairness in why or how death occurs, what governs life and death is not a sense of justice, but of balance. As the Blue Man informs Eddie, "Birth and death are part of a whole" (49). As one person dies, another person is being born. We find similar reflections on life and balance in perhaps the most familiar passage from Ecclesiastes:

> For everything there is a season, and a time for every matter under heaven:
>> a time to be born, and a time to die;
>> a time to plant, and a time to pluck up what is planted;
>> a time to kill, and a time to heal;
>> a time to break down, and a time to build up.
> (Eccl. 3:1–3)

---

[5]Towner, 284.

Similarly to the Blue Man, this section of Ecclesiastes asserts that life and death are part of the fabric that makes up life, that all the things that happen to us are part of the seasons of life. Again, for Ecclesiastes justice is not the issue. Plucking up, killing, breaking down, weeping, mourning, refraining from embracing, losing, throwing away, tearing, hating, fighting war—all elements we might question as unjust or unfair— have an appropriate time in the world of Ecclesiastes. This is a description of how life is, not how it ought to be.

Ecclesiastes does use the language of justice, Hebrew *mispat*. Humans have a place where justice should be mediated, but there Ecclesiastes finds only wickedness (3:16). A person may well see justice and rights denied, but this should not cause surprise. It is only part of a system of human supervisors (5:8). Ecclesiastes repeats the proverbial saying that "the wise mind will know the time and way (*mishpat*)" (8:5), only to follow it immediately with "the troubles of mortals lie heavy upon them" (8:6). This is true because "they do not know what is to be" (8:7). Wisdom should point to the right and just way of life, but human trouble and ignorance of the future counterbalance wisdom's advantage.

In 11:9 and perhaps in the other occurrences of *mispat* in Ecclesiastes, the term refers not so much to justice as to the just judgment that people endure. In chapter 2 the Teacher writing the book encourages people to seek joy and happiness. The author of Ecclesiastes provides exhibit number one for the path of joy and laughter. Vanity is again the test result. The work required to gain joy does not justify the results. Pleasure as the only reward is not reward enough. Still he must conclude,

> I know that there is nothing better for them than to be happy and enjoy themselves as long as they live. (Eccl. 3:12)

Given life's limits and divine sovereignty, joy and pleasure are the preferred goals for earthly living. Moreover, such joy and pleasure are part of the sovereign will:

It is God's gift that all should eat and drink and take pleasure in all their toil. (Eccl. 3:13; compare 5:19)

Human work and toil become part of that joy (3:22), for that is the human lot in life (5:18). That is the way God keeps people occupied (5:20; compare 8:15). Such joy is not eternal, however, for days of darkness replace it (11:8). That is, joy should occupy life however long it lasts, for the next stage is death's darkness.

So in 11:9 Ecclesiastes warns readers of the divine limits that will eventually bring judgment on one who acts for selfish attainment. The book's epilogue repeats the emphasis on God's judgment. Thus Ecclesiastes maintains a tight rein on both sides of his thinking. Joy and happiness are the goal of human freedom, but divine judgment displays God's ultimate control and sovereignty. Life must be lived in view of the two extremes, with no certainty of how to reach the joyous middle way. People on God's earth must simply recognize that each event and emotion of life has its place, a place established by divine sovereignty but revealed to no human mediator.

The Blue Man also reveals that the rhythmic connections of our lives are not the work of a cool, ironic God who finds amusement in a web of human triumph and tragedy. Instead these connections are core to our shared humanity:

"I still don't understand," Eddie whispered. "What good came from your death?"

"You lived," the Blue Man answered.

"But we barely knew each other. I might as well have been a stranger."

The Blue Man put his arms on Eddie's shoulders. Eddie felt that warm, melting sensation.

"Strangers," the Blue Man said, "are just family you have yet to come to know." (*Five People*, 49)

Despite the declaration in Ecclesiastes that all is vanity, some of its teachings deal with the centrality of relationships in life, though with all the fatalism characteristic of "The Teacher." While an individual who lives a solitary life has no one with whom to share his or her workload or accomplishments, those who live in relationship and community find companionship, solace, and perhaps even cause for celebration:

> Two are better than one, because they have a good reward for their toil. For if they fall, one will lift up the other; but woe to one who is alone and falls and does not have another to help. Again, if two lie together, they keep warm; but how can one keep warm alone? And though one might prevail against another, two will withstand one. A threefold cord is not quickly broken. (Eccl. 4:9–12)

Certainly the teachings about human nature that the Blue Man imparts evidence some differences from the philosophy of Ecclesiastes. Although Ecclesiastes acknowledges the craving for relationship and human contact that we all share, the understanding that the Blue Man reveals to Eddie—that there is something innate that makes us a human family—is missing.

Of course, this may point to the central issue that separates the Blue Man's lesson from the teachings of community in Ecclesiastes. While at the core of Ecclesiastes is the vanity of an impermanent life filled with limited understanding, according to the Blue Man there is nothing vain about life. In fact, "the only time we waste is the time we spend thinking we are alone" (50). Although this may not be an exact contradiction of what we encounter in Ecclesiastes, the optimism that is part of the Blue Man's message is certainly missing from Ecclesiastes. While community is an innate part of life—and death—for Albom's character, Ecclesiastes teaches that death is certain. The vanity of life can be improved by living in community and reaching for joy, and all this may make life less of a vain farce, but such happiness is relative, considering the instability of life.

Conclusion

As we journey through Mitch Albom's vision of heaven and initiate a conversation between the teachings of his characters and the teachings of the wisdom traditions, we discover that not everything his characters teach Eddie about heaven has an exact parallel in the wisdom traditions. We have begun a conversation between Albom's vision and the vision of this strange book, Ecclesiastes. Although they do not all fit together, many of the themes of each book are tangential to themes of the other, raising interesting questions about how we, as readers of both Albom's book and of the Bible, see life. Do we opt for the thorny fatalism of Ecclesiastes or the optimism and hope for human connectedness that the Blue Man offers? Does Ecclesiastes trump Albom because we claim that the Bible is spiritually authoritative? How do we deal with the seeming contradiction between the divine sovereign's demand for obedience and human freedom's search for joy? Does Albom leave room for the search for joy during your life? Must all understanding and joy come with a final visit in heaven?

To travel alongside Eddie through heaven means that we have to at least consider such questions. But is all wisdom as troubling and uneven as that offered in Ecclesiastes? Will there always be a tension between the wisdom literature and Albom's vision? We turn now to the Captain and to the ancient scribes of Israel as we continue our journey.

QUESTIONS FOR DISCUSSION

1. How do you see Ecclesiastes as differing from other biblical books? Is its message at all disconcerting?
2. Is it a gift to have your life explained for you after you have lived it, or is it another sort of vanity to have to wait until after death to make sense of things?
3. Do you see Ecclesiastes as a book that contradicts itself? What positive message do you get from reading Ecclesiastes?

4. What role does human freedom and the search for joy have in Ecclesiastes?

5. Does Eddie's life as far as we have seen it indicate that joy just is not in the cards on this earth prior to death? Or does Albom point to human relationships as a source of joy?

For Further Reading

Garret, Duane A. *Proverbs, Ecclesiastes, Song of Songs.* The New American Commentary. Volume 14. Nashville: Broadman and Holman, 1993.

Moore, David George. *Ecclesiastes.* Holman Old Testament Commentary. Volume 14. Nashville: Broadman and Holman, 2003.

Murphy, Roland. *Ecclesiastes.* Word Biblical Commentary. Volume 23A. Dallas: Word Books, 1992.

The New Interpreter's Bible. Volume 5. Nashville: Abingdon Press, 1997. Volume includes commentary on Ecclesiastes.

CHAPTER TWO

proverbs and the captain

"That's the thing. Sometimes when you sacrifice something precious, you're not really losing it. You're just passing it on to someone else."

—CAPTAIN (*FIVE PEOPLE*, 94)

*Just as water reflects the face,
    so one human heart reflects another.*

(PROV. 27:19)

E ddie's meeting with the Captain gives us the second lesson: sacrifice is a part of life. Written large on Albom's pages, ideas of sacrifice encompass nothing so important as life itself. In Eddie's world, lives lost yield second chances and promises kept. This is the lesson the Captain passes on. But how might that inform our own lives, lives that most likely have never seen a battlefield like Eddie's? Moreover, what might the wisdom found in the book of Proverbs have to tell us about sacrifice? Before moving to Albom's text itself, it will be helpful to gain a little perspective about Proverbs.

Proverbial Wisdom: The Right Path

"The early bird gets the worm."

"A penny saved is a penny earned."

"Cleanliness is next to Godliness."

"Look before you leap."

"Haste makes waste."

These bits of traditional wisdom, are familiar to us, comforting even. They provide handy ways of understanding the world, of making sense of life in times of indecision or temptation. While they may contradict one another at times (ever try to be the early bird and look before you leap?) we seem to instinctively know which approaches to use in which situations. One proverb may prove correct in one instance, while another may be called for later on. No single saying holds sway over every aspect of life. While we may not devote much time to analyzing why this is, by acknowledging the truth in all these sayings, these proverbs, we confess to counting on them to provide some sort of framework for our increasingly confusing lives.

This was no less true for ancient Israel. A look at Proverbs will confirm that its wisdom is both vast and varied, so much so that scholars entertain little consensus about many questions arising from Proverbs. The book itself shows a varied history of origins. The subtitles in 1:1; 10:1; 22:17; 24:23; 25:1; 30:1; 31:1 evidence a history of collection, editing, and publication. Different parts of the book were written at different times for different uses with different poetic genres and different types of wisdom within their pages. These discussions reveal that Proverbs is a compilation of various wisdom genres, together revealing some primary truths, not only about life itself but about the ways in which we live out our lives.

Like the Captain, Proverbs wants to suggest that life is full of trade-offs. When presented with choices, we should labor to make the right ones. Indeed, when it comes down to it, we can easily say that for the world of Proverbs, sacrifice can be as simple as daily choosing the right path—the one that serves the Lord, that honors family and friends, and that seeks wisdom continually.

As we explore what this might mean in Albom's world, we turn to four basic themes or types of wisdom found in Proverbs: practical, descriptive, imaginative, and reflective. Through these categories, we will examine the variety of wisdom that comes Eddie's way, always looking for what this might say to us about sacrifice.

Practical Wisdom

> My child, do not walk in [sinners'] way,
> > keep your foot from their paths;
> for their feet run to evil,
> > and they hurry to shed blood. (Prov. 1:15–16)

This sort of wisdom is instructional. It offers tried-and-true rules for thought and action, most often in the form of a lecture or sermon. Ultimately such wisdom has its home in the family, where parents train children. The form is taken over by schools and royal courts to train leaders, the teacher treating students as "sons" or "children." Ultimately this type of wisdom encourages obedience and generally works to create a sense of where the communal priorities and boundaries exist. Practical, instructional wisdom leads the "child" to know how to fit into the different roles in society. It helps society maintain its decorum and stability. It develops a new generation of leaders to uphold the traditions of the nation. It appears most often in Proverbs 1—9 as well as in chapters 30 and 31.

For Eddie instructional wisdom comes in the form of advice for self-preservation. Unlike the ancient Israelite teachings meant to introduce the student to his/her role in the community, the things Eddie learns are meant first and foremost to keep him alive. Mickey Shea's instructions to Eddie in the arcade do just that:

> "Listen to me, lad…War is no game. If there's a shot to be made, you make it, you hear? No guilt. No hesitation. You fire and you fire and you don't think about who

you're shootin' or killin' or why, y'hear me? You want to come home again, you just fire, you don't think…It's the thinking that gets you killed." (*Five People,* 59–60)

If the content of Mickey's advice seems to contradict that espoused in Proverbs 1:15–16, its structure and implications do not. Both are clearly intended to clarify what the hearer must do to preserve him- or herself. The Proverbs student must continue to choose right paths. For Eddie the question centers on what sacrifices may be necessary to simply come home alive. Here he is called to suspend his humanity, his sense that he and the enemy may be the same. This is the only way he can avoid getting killed. In a sense, to serve his country, to protect his physical life, he must be willing to sacrifice his soul. Such a personal sacrifice preserves the freedom of his people to maintain the community traditions and life. From a somewhat different perspective, the student in Proverbs sacrifices what might be called the rights of personal freedom and pleasure to maintain the moral fiber and thus the life of the nation.

Descriptive Wisdom

A cheerful heart is a good medicine,
> but a downcast spirit dries up the bones. (Prov. 17:22)

Rather than lay out explicit expectations, this type of wisdom guides its hearers by implication, positing general truths about a variety of subjects. Found most often in what scholars refer to as the Solomonic Collections (1:1—22:16; 25:1—29:27, those collections traditionally attributed to King Solomon), these two-liners lay bare the nature of the real world. Indeed, such observations as "In all toil there is profit, / but mere talk leads only to poverty" (14:23) reveal a certain dedication to observation and truth-telling that many sociologists might appreciate. Here long years and even generations of experience are boiled down to two lines. These are not intended to be natural laws that always work. They simply suggest what experience has taught to be the best approach to life in different situations a person may face. Righteousness, optimism, fear of God, obedience, caution in speaking, hard work, honesty, wise use of money—these virtues prove to bring hope and purpose in the long run. Opposite behavior lets the community view you as foolish, undisciplined, untrustworthy, dangerous, wicked, and thus a threat to the community.

Speaking of Eddie's sudden and destructive impetus to throw himself into a fire, the Captain says,

> "What happened to you—I've seen it happen before. A soldier reaches a certain point and then he can't go anymore. Sometimes it's in the middle of the night. A man'll just roll out of his tent and start walking, barefoot, half-naked, like he's going home, like he lives just around the corner." (*Five People,* 88)

The Captain engages Eddie in truth-telling, describing for him the nature of men in war, the disillusionment that leads to total abandonment. Like the truth reflected in Proverbs 17:22, in war the downcast spirit can only collapse in upon itself.

For Eddie, what is at stake in this conversation is his truth—he returned home a "different man" (85), depressed and absent, his spirit having succumbed to the baseness of his war. He no longer aspired to be an engineer, settling back into Ruby Pier and allowing his bones to dry up, literally and metaphorically. The Captain becomes the one to tell Eddie the truth not only about his leg but also about himself. "'I took your leg,' the Captain said, quietly, 'to save your life'" (88).

And here we find the crux of the story—Eddie's journey in heaven has wisdom as its purpose, yet the wisdom of truth sears. In hearing the truth from the Captain, in accepting his own part in his life story, Eddie sacrifices his version of reality, which he has relied on to explain his "nothing life" (65). The sacrifice yields grief and disappointment, but it also frees Eddie to know that in the end his life really was his own.

In similar fashion descriptive proverbs call for sacrifice of the person one might choose to become in favor of the person who best serves society, with its corporate identity and goals. Whether it is speaking of a child molding to fit family values or future court officials giving up individual heroics to serve the king's pleasures, Proverbs calls on its students to exercise self-discipline in adhering to society's expectations rather than to develop personal goals and directions.

But Eddie learned the lessons of sacrifice only in his heaven, while Proverbs seeks to direct people to the joys of sacrifice while they are in their earthly life. Eddie had to endure the meaninglessness and lack of hope at Ruby Pier as he sacrificed a life of accomplishment. Albom appears to say that Eddie was fated to such sacrifice. Would Proverbs have encouraged Eddie to optimistic striving for a better place in which to serve his community? Or would Proverbs agree that freedom for hope comes only after this life?

Imaginative Wisdom

> I passed by the field of one who was lazy,
>> by the vineyard of a stupid person;
> and see, it was all overgrown with thorns;
>> the ground was covered with nettles,
>> and its stone wall was broken down.
> Then I saw and considered it;
>> I looked and received instruction.
> A little sleep, a little slumber,
>> a little folding of the hands to rest,
> and poverty will come upon you like a robber,
>> and want, like an armed warrior. (Prov. 24: 30–34)

This type of wisdom appears throughout the book. Unlike descriptive wisdom, however, this wisdom appeals to one's imagination, requiring the hearer to conjure a situation in order to imagine the results should the wrong path be chosen. For example Proverbs 24:30–34, above, assumes a first-person narrative voice as though teaching by parable. It calls on the listener to go back to childhood days on the farm. Remember which farmer's crops proved to be bountiful and which farmer's harvest failed. What explanation do you have for the distinctly different results? Can you learn the difference between self-disciplined hard work and undisciplined laziness? Which produces the desired results? The picture of the different harvests stays in the pupil's head far beyond the teaching hour. Temptation to be lazy is tempered by the teacher's imaginative wisdom. Pictures remain better than a thousand words.

The pictures of imaginative wisdom call for a type of sacrifice, for self-discipline, refusal to be lazy, hard work. Self-discipline leads one to sacrifice energy, time, sweat, and strength to achieve the good of the larger society.

For Eddie, imaginative wisdom arises from the Captain's promise that he would "leave no one behind" (64). The Captain's care for his soldiers is obvious, and he reaps the fruit of that. His soldiers are loyal, believing that he could "keep them alive" (86). For Eddie, counting on the Captain makes fighting easier. He can imagine any number of situations in war, all ending well because the Captain will not leave anyone behind. Such knowledge gives Eddie and his fellow soldiers the courage they need to stand together. Indeed, it gives them the strength necessary to survive.

He couldn't always keep them alive, confesses the Captain. But his promise gives the soldiers something to believe in, something to hold on to. In the end, it is this promise that compels the Captain to shoot Eddie and to scout the way for those in the jeep. In keeping the promise, the Captain unknowingly sacrifices his own life. Interestingly, what we might see as a rather huge sacrifice, the Captain sees as an everyday aspect of life:

> "Sacrifice is a part of life. It's *supposed* to be. It's not something to regret. It's something to *aspire* to. Little sacrifices. Big sacrifices. A mother works so her son

can go to school. A daughter moves home to take care of her sick father." (*Five People,* 93)

It's all the same, the Captain implies. We can easily imagine either of these scenarios, but they hardly seem on a par with death. And yet ultimately, that is exactly what the Captain hopes to communicate—that sacrifices happen every day, and it is up to us to make our own peace with that.

Both Albom and imaginative wisdom call for sacrifice. For Albom, sacrifice is what you expect to receive, what is normal and cannot be avoided. Imaginative wisdom calls for a decision to sacrifice. Sacrifice becomes a life value one elects to adopt or reject. For the Captain his personal sacrifice is a by-product of living out of his imaginative wisdom. He bows to life's fate as he sticks to his principled promise. For the "Solomonic" wisdom, sacrifice comes as one listens to imagination, remembers the imagined, and draws consequences from it. It can lead to positive choices to act in self-disciplined ways and negative choices to refuse to follow false paths (see Prov. 7:6–27).

Reflective Wisdom

> For whoever finds me finds life
> and obtains favor from the LORD. (Prov. 8:35)

Finally, we must understand that some wisdom cannot be fully transmitted by means of a pithy saying. Rather, some knowledge can only be born of true desire and hard work. Indeed, attaining a sense of the profound, instilling that which pushes the bounds of human comprehension, requires a serious commitment to thought and study. This idea proves to be one of the central themes of Proverbs. The pursuit of wisdom is integral to living a productive life. Moreover, Proverbs 8:1–36 takes that urging to a higher level by personifying Wisdom with a female voice and portraying her as the first creative act of God and therefore highly prized.

"The LORD created me at the beginning of his work,
   the first of his acts of long ago.
Ages ago I was set up,
   at the first, before the beginning of the earth.
When there were no depths I was brought forth,
   when there were no springs abounding with water.
Before the mountains had been shaped,
   before the hills, I was brought forth—
when he had not yet made earth and fields,
   or the world's first bits of soil.
When he established the heavens, I was there,
   when he drew a circle on the face of the deep,
when he made firm the skies above,
   when he established the fountains of the deep,
when he assigned to the sea its limit,
   so that the waters might not transgress his command,
when he marked out the foundations of the earth,
   then I was beside him, like a master worker;
and I was daily his delight,
   rejoicing before him always,
rejoicing in his inhabited world
   and delighting in the human race.
And now, my children, listen to me:
   happy are those who keep my ways.
Hear instruction and be wise,
   and do not neglect it." (Prov. 8:22–33)

Within this chapter, Wisdom clearly emerges as a human role model, a yardstick against which one measures one's own capacity for understanding. The pursuit of wisdom, the process of internalizing the call of Lady Wisdom, is at once the worship and pursuit of Divine nature, of God's true self.

Again wisdom literature encourages the student to work. This work is more mental and even spiritual than physical. One must find the very nature of creation itself. One must see the intellectual, wise component that binds all creation together.

Having learned the very essence of the created order, the student must work to adapt a personal lifestyle to fit into that order. To fail to do so is to be foolish, ignorant, and disorderly.

In a sense, reflective wisdom encapsulates Albom's entire project. To be sure, diligent pursuit of knowledge requires that Eddie struggle with the person before him and come away with a higher level of understanding. "You followin' this?" (92) the Captain wants to know. Yes, it seems Eddie is following. As his second encounter draws to a close, Eddie finds himself catching on, and yet still he searches for something more. "'Wait,' Eddie yelled. 'I gotta know something. My death. At the pier. Did I save that girl?'"(96). He catches himself, believing that the question is somehow out of place and yet powerless to keep from asking. As the Captain walks away, Eddie knows so much more about himself, but he still desires to know—did his life, his sacrifice, make a difference?

Thus wisdom and Albom both posit sacrifice as an essential element of life. The lesson of sacrifice is learned through various types of wisdom. But a vast chasm separates Eddie's and the Captain's sacrifices from those wisdom calls the student to make. According to Albom, sacrifices occur as normal, virtually inescapable parts of life. The one making the sacrifice often is unaware of the sacrifice and quite unable to understand the meaning of sacrifice until stops in heaven reveal the ultimate purpose and results.

The wise student makes sacrifices knowingly. Sacrifice is a lifestyle choice that places community before individual. It is an intellectual choice to align one's self with the order of the universe instead of with the disorder of fools. Sacrifice is not something that suddenly happens to the individual. Sacrifice is the result of an endeavor to understand the universe, its order, its purposes, and its Creator. Albom with his silence about the Divine apparently has no room for such intentional sacrifice.

QUESTIONS FOR DISCUSSION

1. What do you think of when you hear the word *sacrifice*? Are there limits to how you can define it?
2. After thinking about the different kinds of wisdom offered in Proverbs, in what category would you place the wisdom that you feel the most comfortable receiving? Why?
3. Proverbs speaks only in passing about God. Yet it makes the "fear of the LORD" the center of its call for sacrifice and the created order the model for personal sacrifice. How do these two elements enter into your daily decisions to sacrifice present energy, pleasure, and time for long-term or societal goals?
4. Do you agree that sacrifice is a central theme for Albom? How do you think Albom would define sacrifice?
5. Does one really sacrifice in Albom's world, which seems driven by fate, or is sacrifice only seen looking backward from heaven?
6. What role does sacrifice play in your own life? What motivates you to sacrifice? What is it that you actually give up as you sacrifice? Does your understanding of heaven play a role in your choosing to or not to sacrifice?

FOR FURTHER READING

Dell, Katharine. *Get Wisdom, Get Insight: An Introduction to Israel's Wisdom Literature*. Macon, Ga.: Smyth & Helwys, 2000.

Melchert, Charles. *Wise Teaching: Biblical Wisdom and Educational Ministry*. Harrisburg, Pa.: Trinity Press, 1998.

The New Interpreter's Bible. Volume 5. Nashville: Abingdon Press, 1997.

CHAPTER THREE

ruby, eddie, and his old man

Eddie never said this—not to his wife, not to his mother, not to anyone—but he cursed his father for dying and for trapping him in the very life he'd been trying to escape; a life that, as he heard the old man laughing from the grave, apparently now was good enough for him.

(*Five People*, 128)

Commit your way to the Lord;
    trust in him, and he will act.
He will make your vindication shine like the light
    and the justice of your cause like the noonday.

(Ps. 37:5–6)

As Eddie continues his celestial quest, heaven begins to take a familiar shape.

A diner.

So far heaven has failed to live up to Eddie's expectation of a paradise marked by streets paved with gold. It has been a strange place, filled with revelations that have challenged the way Eddie looks at his own life. Now, instead of offering the heavenly feast that so many parables and prophecies seem to promise, it looks strikingly similar to the roadside eateries in which Eddie has taken many meals:

> They all looked the same—high-backed booths, shiny countertops, a row of small-paned windows across the front, which, from the outside, made customers appear like riders in railroad car. (*Five People,* 99–100)

When he looks inside, Eddie discovers that most of the patrons at the diner are wounded—arms missing, faces scarred.

They are served food that looks beautiful and tasty, meals that can only be described as heavenly. Among the diners, to Eddie's chagrin, sits his father, hunched over a table in a booth, completely oblivious to Eddie's repeated shouts.

But Eddie's father is not the third person that Eddie meets in heaven. The third person Eddie meets has something to tell him about his father. She is an old woman, but not just any old woman. She is the beloved wife of an industrialist who built an amusement park in her honor, the very same park where Eddie worked and met his end. She is the Ruby of Ruby Pier.

She tells Eddie the tale of her life. She and her husband, Emile, fell in love. Her husband, the risk-taking investor, amassed a fortune, then lost nearly all of it, as well as his vigor for life. Near the end of her husband's life, he shared a hospital room with Eddie's father. For Ruby, this was a discovery that would compound her regret that Ruby Pier had ever been built.

She reveals to Eddie the shocking circumstances surrounding the death of Eddie's father. Evidently his father saved Mickey Shea—a family friend who had earlier assaulted Eddie's mother—from drowning. As a result Eddie's father contracted the pneumonia that killed him. At the time of his death, Eddie's father ached with regret for shutting himself off from the love of his family:

> "Sometime during the night, your father awakened. He rose from his bed, staggered across the room, and found the strength to raise the window sash. He called your mother's name with what little voice he had, and he called yours, too, and your brother, Joe. And he called for Mickey." (*Five People,* 139–40)

After revealing this to Eddie, Ruby leaves him with a lesson about forgiveness that he must put into play. But is forgiveness ever easy, even in heaven? To examine this issue, we will now take a look at a selection of poems that are sometimes considered part of the wisdom tradition. We turn now to the book of Psalms.

The Poetry of Life

We cannot prove the popular theory that the book of Psalms includes examples of wisdom literature. Several psalms do exhibit themes and styles similar to those of wisdom literature. Still, scholars find many other dominant themes to use in categorizing psalms. Thus, many critical scholars consider it a considerable leap of faith to trace the origin of any of the Psalms to the wisdom theology of the scribes.

Traditionally psalms have been described in the following way: As Hebrew poetry, they functioned as part of the liturgical life of ancient Israel. This poetry not only expressed the agony and ecstasy of the community gathered for worship but also served a didactic purpose. Often it described the nature of God (Ps. 46), commenting on the human condition vis-à-vis humanity's relationship to God (Ps. 55), or reminding worshipers of their ancestors' experiences during traumatic periods such as the Babylonian exile (Ps. 137).

Scholarly analysis isolates five major types of psalms:

1. *Royal psalms,* which deal with Israel's kingship and become seen as messianic psalms pointing to the future—Psalms 2, 18, 20, 21, 28, 45, 61, 63, 72, 89, 101, 110, 132.
2. *Hymns or songs of praise to YHWH*—Psalms 8, 19, 29, 33, 65, 100, 103, 105, 111, 113, 114, 117, 135, 136, 145—150.
3. *Individual laments or songs of supplication*—Psalms 3—7, 13, 17, 22, 25, 26, 28, 35, 38—43, 51, 54—57, 61, 63, 64, 69—71, 77, 83, 86, 88, 94, 102, 109, 126, 130, 134, 140—144.
4. *Individual thanksgiving songs*—Psalms 9—10, 18, 30—32, 34, 66, 92, 107, 116, 118, 120, 124, 129, 138, 139.
5. *Communal laments*—Psalms 12, 44, 60, 74, 79, 80, 85, 90, 123, 137.

Wisdom psalms thus form a minor category in the Psalter. Whereas other categories find definition from formal and linguistic elements appearing in most examples of the genre, wisdom psalms find definition by their function, namely that of bringing instruction. Included in this group are Psalms 1, 14, 36, 37, 49, 53, 73, 78, 112, 119, 127, 128, 133.

We are most interested in Psalms 37, 49, 73, 112, and 127. Although they certainly exhibit many of the characteristics of the lament, they are perhaps better described as *aphoristic*. They are meditative poems concerned with the problem of suffering, particularly the suffering of the righteous. As we have seen in Ecclesiastes and Proverbs, and as we will see in our examination of Job, this is a major theme of wisdom literature.

To say that this group of psalms deals with wisdom themes and serves didactic functions does not mean they originate with teachers who have nothing to do with the cultic worship, in contrast to more ritualistic psalms that originated with priests and other cultic officials. Indeed, Erhard Gerstenberger has recently argued that the distinction is not cult versus school. Rather it is preexilic cult versus postexilic cult:

> Israel's social and political structure had changed. We have to visualize communities of Jews scattered all over the world, no longer enjoying the protection of their native state. Instead, the leaders—mostly scribes and Levites—tried to gather members and proselytes around the written Word of God. These early Jewish communities fought against religious extermination, insisting on the one, exclusive, and invisible God, on his *tora*, on his Sabbath, and on his stipulations concerning food, marriage, and all the other matters of daily life. They hoped for the restitution of the Davidic empire and God's revenge upon all oppressors. To maintain such a dynamic tradition the Jews studied the written heritage of their ancestors. Teaching this revealed will of God became the very backbone of communal and individual existence. At this point wisdom influence entered Jewish life, and most of all, Jewish cult...A well-informed, theologically versed leader presents

the psalm to a listening congregation. The general tone of wisdom psalms is that of pastoral counseling.... The obvious aim was the edification and orientation of the members of the synagogal community.[1]

Obviously a major theme of such wisdom-oriented worship would be the undeserved fate of the suffering exiles. This theme of the reasonableness (or unreasonableness) of suffering is one of the major parallels that has drawn us to wisdom literature in our examination of Albom's book. The wisdom psalms' thematic similarities make them illuminating tools for our look at the broken relationship between Eddie and his father.

Forgiving a Father

For Eddie, loving his father was always difficult work. His father was never affectionate, often violent. Whenever Eddie had shared his dreams—of becoming an engineer, for example—his father would always sneer and demand to know why the life he lived was not good enough for his son.

Not long after Eddie returned injured from the war, he sank into a debilitating depression. Then the tense nature of the relationship with his father finally exploded. After a night of drinking, his father came home, demanding that Eddie get a job. As he had so many times before, his father swung at him. This time Eddie, much stronger than he ever was as a teenager and finally fed up with everything that had happened to him over the years, did something he had never done when his father would assault him—he defended himself.

Utterly shocked, Eddie's father never spoke to him again. Then, when Eddie was thirty-three, his father died after a long struggle in the hospital. For the rest of his life, Eddie believed that his father's death had been the result of one of his infamous

---

[1]Erhard S. Gerstenberger, *Psalms Part 1 with an Introduction to Cultic Poetry*, The Forms of the Old Testament Literature, vol. 14 (Grand Rapids: Eerdmans, 1988), 20–21.

drinking binges. While his father was incapacitated, Eddie assumed many of his father's responsibilities, both in taking care of his mother and at the Pier. Of course he resented having to do this, and this resentment grew over the years after his father died. Eddie grew to believe that his lot in life had been his father's ultimate revenge for Eddie's dreams of bettering his lot in life. Eddie believed that his father must be spending eternity gloating that his drunken demise landed Eddie in the same dead-end job that he had held for so long.

One of the wisdom psalms, Psalm 37, offers some interesting advice concerning anger and resentment:

Refrain from anger, and forsake wrath.
    Do not fret—it leads only to evil.
For the wicked shall be cut off,
    but those who wait for the LORD shall inherit the land.
    (Ps. 37:8–9)

This psalm is in many ways an interesting hybrid, reflecting both the cause-and-effect theology that dominates Proverbs and the covenantal theology of much of the Hebrew Bible. Life is ordered by YHWH, the psalm asserts—trust in the way of YHWH, adhere to the divine order of things, and you will be blessed (compare Prov. 8). Evoking the covenantal promise of a homeland, the psalm asserts that those who are motivated by wickedness and do not follow the way of YHWH will receive no such reward. We can see the exiled Jewish worshipers biting their tongues as the worship leader instructs them in how to deal with anger and resentment. They did not face a dead father. They faced foreign rulers, enemies, every day. Worship played on the theme of God's promises and God's miraculous deliverance of the chosen people. But the exiles experienced none of this. Waiting for the Lord in a foreign land required a bit more than most of them could do (compare Ps. 137). Empowered foreigners ruled their lives. What did they have to wait for? All the pastoral counseling they could do was listen to one another's complaints and let one another vent their anger. Why should they "refrain from anger and forsake wrath"?

Psalm 37 offers several reasons. The wicked enemies will soon disappear (vv. 2, 9–10, 15, 20, 35–36, 38). Good deeds will be rewarded (vv. 3, 5, 18–19). God's meek (that is, not angry or vindictive) people will own the land (vv. 3, 9, 11, 22, 34), living in it forever (v. 29, 37). God will protect the righteous (vv. 17, 23–24, 33, 39–40). They have God's law or *torah* to guide them (v. 31). Here the explicit call to forgive does not occur, simply the call to faith in God and to refraining from anger.

Psalm 49 points the angry exiles in another direction. They must recognize their own mortality and make the most of life while they have it. They must confess that they continue to live only because God rescues them. Indeed, Psalm 49 offers one of the Old Testament's few traces of hope for life beyond the grave (v. 15). The enemies' wealth and power thus do not make them better than exiled, powerless Jewish worshipers. They, too, will soon die, as do all people.

Following worship's wisdom instruction is never easy. The writer/teacher behind Psalm 73 confesses his envy at the prosperity of the wicked (vv. 2–3). Even God seems not to know the acts and attitudes of the wicked (vv. 10–12). Nor does God appear to reward the righteous (vv. 13–14). Worship changes the perspective, revealing the mortality of the wicked (vv. 17–20). This revelation turns the psalmist back to trust in God for the present and the future (v. 24). Earth's riches do not bring envy any longer, for God has become the only desire (v. 25). Again the release from envy and hatred is experienced with God in worship and telling all God's acts (v. 28). No word about forgiveness appears.

Psalm 112 turns the tables on Psalm 37, our starting point. Praise and worship join faithfulness to God's commandments to bring assurance for the psalmist, while the enemies express anger and lose all they have. Bad news does not alarm God's faithful people. Still, however, we find no explicit word of forgiveness.

Finally, Psalm 127 calls on people able to rebuild their house, God's temple. It calls for their families to trust in God or their labor will be in vain. Anxiety accomplishes nothing. Trust in God brings sleep, rest, and happiness. These wisdom psalms, along with most of the Old Testament, call on the audience to resist anger and resentment. But these psalms and the rest of the Old Testament seldom, if ever, call readers to forgive another person.

Eddie, in his resentment, clearly believes that his father's abuse and irresponsibility have ruined his life. Does Psalm 37 vindicate him? Does it, in its insistence that those who commit wickedness will "get theirs in the end," provide Eddie with an adequate promise that it is not his father who will get vindication from beyond the grave, but Eddie who gets the last laugh?

Not exactly. Although the psalm certainly promises vindication for the righteous and punishment for the wicked, one of the reasons it is considered wisdom literature is because it contains an element of moral instruction. Righteousness cannot be assumed by those who are bitterly awaiting the destruction of their enemies:

> The mouths of the righteous utter wisdom,
>   and their tongues speak justice.
> The law of their God is in their hearts;
>   their steps do not slip. (Ps. 37:30–31)

Indeed, to be righteous is to live in accordance with the way of YHWH, not to allow oneself to be bogged down by desire for vengeance. After all, the desire for vengeance may be the fine line that separates the righteous from the wicked:

> The wicked watch for the righteous,
>   and seek to kill them. (Ps. 37:32)

The advice of the psalm is double-edged—do not worry about those persons who are wicked, not only because YHWH will deal with them but also because by fretting about them and harboring hatred for them, it is easy to fall into the same traps of wickedness. "Do not fret because of the wicked; / do not be envious of wrongdoers" (37:1) because it is too easy for one's envy to be fulfilled.

In that regard, some of Ruby's final words to Eddie are quite psalmlike:

> "Holding anger is a poison. It eats you from inside. We think that hating is a weapon that attacks the person who harmed us. But hatred is a curved blade. And the harm we do, we do to ourselves." (*Five People,* 141)

Eddie thus learns his next lesson—forgiveness is not about letting someone off the hook for his or her transgressions. Forgiveness is honestly confronting the pain we feel and that we cause so that we may be able to heal and continue to grow. Although Ruby is the third person Eddie meets in heaven, he cannot move on immediately after she leaves. Instead he has to at last forgive his father. He expresses his forgiveness in a language they can both understand:

> His voice wobbled until it was high and wailing, not his own anymore. "OK? YOU HEAR ME?" he screamed. Then softer: "You hear me? Dad?" He leaned in close. He saw his father's dirty hands. He spoke the last familiar words in a whisper. "It's fixed." (*Five People,* 144)

Conclusion

This stop along Eddie's journey through heaven contains some of Albom's most emotionally affective writing. Most of us have had an experience with a loved one whose hurtful actions we find difficult to forgive. For many of us the regret and bitterness we feel are magnified by the deaths of the people who cause us pain. For us and for Eddie, forgiveness is a liberating experience, one that frees us from some of the baggage that can weigh us down for much of our lives.

In looking at how the wisdom psalms can enter into this conversation, we have developed another layer in our discussion. The writers of these psalms say that not becoming weighed down by the deeds of those who hurt us greatly affects our relationship with God. To resist the temptation to hold on to anger and resentment is to grow in faith and to grow in wisdom. Yet the Old Testament passages do not expressly call for persons to forgive those who have treated them wickedly and destructively. Eddie's problem is in personal relations. The Psalms speak more generally of the community's response to political and economic issues. The individual must learn not to take on the nation's burdens and let strong feelings of opposing national enemies steal the joys of living. This applies even to the individual who daily faces the discomfort and harm that national captors bring. Economic and political oppression do not give one leave to let hatred and anger dominate life. Rather, trust in God and hope for the future should bring one to righteous living and personal experience of divine protection. In the wisdom tradition Sirach calls on the student to "forgive your neighbor the wrong he has done, / and then your sins will be pardoned when you pray. / Does anyone harbor anger against another, / and expect healing from the Lord? / If one has no mercy toward another like himself, / can he then seek pardon for his own sins? / If a mere mortal harbors wrath, / who will make an atoning sacrifice for his sins?" (Sir. 28:2).

Only with Jesus do we get the call to forgive one's enemies. Such forgiveness is based on receiving love and forgiveness from God and thus being able to love as well as forgive one's enemies (Mt. 5:43–47; compare Lk. 6:35–37; Rom. 12:14–21). Jesus not only taught such forgiveness (Mt. 5:7; 6:12–15; 18:15–22; Lk. 11:4; 17:3–4; compare Eph. 4:32; Col. 3:13) but also practiced it (Lk. 23:34).

We thus find forgiveness set forth in different ways, one might even say different stages, in our comparison of Eddie with the wisdom tradition. Wisdom begins by leading away from anger and hatred. Eddie gets things fixed with his father. Sirach ties being forgiven and having sins atoned for to forgiving a neighbor and having mercy on the other person. Jesus calls for love for the enemy, forgiveness for the enemy, and practices what he preaches.

The next person whom Eddie meets reminds him of one of the deepest, most compelling emotions that has been part of his life: Love. To discuss love and Eddie's long devotion to his wife, Marguerite, we need not look far in the wisdom literature to find a conversation partner. We need only to look at the great love poem of the Hebrew Bible: Song of Solomon (or The Song of Songs).

QUESTIONS FOR DISCUSSION

1. Take a look at the psalms considered to have wisdom qualities. Do they look similar to other wisdom books? Why or why not?
2. Whom does forgiveness serve more, the one who is forgiven or the person doing the forgiving?
3. What does Psalm 37 tell you about ethical behavior and your relationship with God?
4. What causes anger and resentment to erupt in your life? How do you handle such eruptions?
5. What is the relationship between Eddie's situation with his father and the exiled Jews' situation with their captors? What can you learn from each situation?
6. What is the relationship between refraining from anger, having mercy, forgiving, and loving? Must one experience forgiveness before being able to forgive? Can one forgive someone without loving the person?

CHAPTER FOUR

the song of solomon and marguerite

"Lost love is still love, Eddie. It takes a different form, that's all."

—MARGUERITE (*FIVE PEOPLE*, 173)

Set me as a seal upon your heart,
*   as a seal upon your arm;*
for love is strong as death,
*   passion fierce as the grave.*
Its flashes are flashes of fire,
*   a raging flame.*

(SONG 8:6)

" I lost the only woman I ever loved," admits Eddie, overwhelmed by Marguerite's presence (173). And so Eddie receives his fourth lesson in heaven—that love lives beyond mere physical presence, that love encompasses not only our hearts and souls but also our most cherished memories. In short, that love lives even when we do not. As we look at what Albom has to say about love, it seems appropriate to examine what the Bible's most famous book of love has to say to us as well. At this point it is important to remember that neither one of these texts were written to reflect on the other. Any time we see common themes or ideas it is because we have, to a certain extent, wanted to see them. We impose our twenty-first century ideas about love, those perhaps contained in Albom's work, on the Song of Solomon. To this extent, these texts will not agree on everything, nor do they explicitly echo each other. Instead our analysis will only concentrate on two to three ideas, ideas that each text covers in its own way.

The Song of Solomon

Known in the Hebrew text as The Song of Songs, this particular book poses an inordinate number of questions for scholars and laity alike. In a collection of works recounting the history of God's works among and for God's people, Song of Solomon seems peculiarly out of place.

What is this book about? Why include it in the Bible? What wisdom does it actually offer? Renita Weems vividly describes the experience of reading the Song:

> To open the pages of this brief volume of poetry is to leave the world of exceptional heroism, tribal conflict, political disputes, royal intrigue, religious reforms, and divine judgment and to enter the world of domestic relations, private sentiments, and interpersonal discourse. Filled with language of sensuality, longing, intimacy, playfulness, and human affection, Song of Songs introduces the reader to the non-public world of ancient Israel. The relationships are private (i.e., a man and a woman), the conversation is between intimates (e.g., "darling,""beloved," "friend"), and the language hints of kinship bonds (e.g., mother, sister, brother, daughter). At last, readers of Scripture have the opportunity to focus not so much on the external politics that organized and dominated the lives of Hebrew people (e.g., palace intrigue, temple politics, prophetic conflict, international doom, natural disasters) but on the internal systems and attitudes that also shaped the lives of the people of Israel."[1]

To be sure, Song of Solomon is about as racy a text as one can find between the covers of the Bible. Its eight chapters of poetry never once refer to God. The poems seem intent on celebrating the physical realities of love rather than the mighty

---

[1] Renita J. Weems, "Song of Songs," in *New Interpreter's Bible,* vol. 5 (Nashville: Abingdon Press, 1979), 363.

acts of Yahweh or the illustrious history of Israelite warriors. Indeed, it is quite different from anything else we find in wisdom literature, or in the Bible as a whole. As we discussed in chapter 2 with Proverbs, the attribution to Solomon is a later addition to the work, meant to confer a level of authority rather than actual authorship. As Weems states: "Attributing the love poems to Solomon probably represents an attempt by the scribes to associate the work with the wisest and most notorious king in Israel's history. Appending his name to the book would place it foremost within an intellectual stream of respected and authoritative theological reflection, the wisdom tradition."[2] If not Solomon, then who and when? Roland Murphy gives the terse answer: "the date of the work cannot be ascertained."[3] Marvin Pope's explanation is on target: "The dating game as played with biblical books like Job and the Song of Songs, as well as with many of the Psalms, remains imprecise and the score is difficult to compute. There are grounds for both the oldest and the youngest estimates."[4]

Scholars often begin their work with Song of Solomon by being sensitive to genre. It is first and foremost poetry, initially composed orally, so that the transfer to the page makes commentary a cumbersome task at best. Changing tenses and speakers creates confusion about point of view, while strange references make the subject matter hard to discern. Scholars typically fall into one of two camps when reviewing all these factors: either they believe it to be a whole text with a specific

---

[2]Renita J. Weems, *What Matters Most: Ten Lessons in Living Passionately from the Song of Solomon* (West Bloomfield, Mich.: Warner Books with Walk Worthy Press, 2004.), 365. Note, however, the arguments of Duane Garrett, *Song of Songs,* Word Biblical Commentary, vol. 23B (Nashville: Thomas Nelson Publishers, 2004), 16–22, concluding that "the Hebrew of the Song of Songs in no way demands a Persian or Hellenistic provenance for the text. The imagery used in the Song suggests a pan-Israelite viewpoint and composition by a poet who had direct experience with wealth and exotic luxuries, and this fits well with a provenance in the Solomonic empire...Thus the evidence converges on this conclusion: the book was written during the united monarchy." Weems, 371, agrees that "the archaic grammatical and linguistic forms found in the book suggest that some version of the book dates back to the early period in Israel's history."

[3]"Song of Songs, Book of," *The Anchor Bible Dictionary,* vol. 6 (New York: Doubleday, 1992), 150)

[4]*Song of Songs,* Anchor Bible, vol. 7C (Garden City, N.Y.: Doubleday, 1977), 27.

plot and purpose, or they think of it as a collection of poems intended for a spectrum of uses. Duane Garrett, for example, sees a unified structure, including thirteen songs by a single poet, creating a literary piece with analogies in other cultures.[5] Weems argues on the other side that "finding a uniform structure and consistent pattern to the book's content is not always possible. Those who perceive any literary unity to the poetry usually argue on the basis of their own aesthetic insights and not on the basis of any straightforward criteria."[6]

Depending on which camp they fall into, commentators speculate on uses and meaning that support their assumptions about the text's structure. If they assume that the book is simply a collection of love lyrics, they are more likely to suppose it was a cycle of marriage poems. On the flip side, if scholars assume the book to be a complete story, they most often believe it to be a dramatic performance of some kind, most likely a seasonal fertility ritual meant to join the deity and the human in a bid for an abundant harvest.

Beyond the structure argument the traditional interpretation still has adherents. For these people Song of Solomon is an allegory expressing God's love for Israel or Christ's love for the church. This has long been the standard interpretation of Song of Solomon, offered as a way of avoiding the implications were we to read it literally. If read as an allegory in which either Israel or the church plays the part of the maiden, the book becomes much more acceptable as sacred scripture.

Finally, Song of Solomon offers many critics interested in women's voices a text with which to play. While the object of Song is the maiden's male lover, the text itself is written in a female voice and from a female perspective with only the occasional interruption from the Shepherd himself. Feminist commentators tend to understand the book as a whole and see in it a progression of consciousness. They posit that the

---

[5]Garrett, 26. He even devises a complex chiastic structure for the entire Song (32).
[6]Weems, *What Matters Most,* 372.

Shulammite, the only name given the speaker, moves from being a naïve young woman caught up in the passion of love to a wiser, more mature woman, who has learned the lessons, both negative and positive, that love teaches. Some go so far as to claim that in the end the writer has, in the voice of the Shulammite, subverted traditional gender expectations and asserted ownership of her own sexuality.

Whether any of this reflects an author's intention is moot—ultimately what is important here is how we read it and what we can take away from it.

> "This music, performed over centuries and for generations, was created to charm audiences through its use of erotic allusions, veiled speeches, and extravagant imagery. Indeed, in the Song of Songs, audiences are at least implicitly invited to assume the identities of the lovers, to identify with their plight, to sympathize with their dilemma, to share their resolve, to relish their tenacity, to enjoy their clever disguises, to mourn their losses and flaws, to celebrate their joys and strength, and to endure with them unto the end."[7]

So what might we as readers take away from a comparison of Albom's story about Eddie and Marguerite with Song of Solomon? What do these texts tell us about love? As we noted above, each text has multiple things to say on the subject. For our purposes, I want to suggest three ways of getting at the wisdom about love that both books impart: (1) that love is specific; (2) that love is cyclical, enduring both dormant and fertile times; and (3) that love has multiple forms.

Love Is Specific

What people find then is a *certain* love. And Eddie found a certain love with Marguerite, a grateful love, a deep

---

[7]Ibid., in reference to Roland Murphy, *The Song of Songs*, Hermeneia (Minneapolis: Fortress Press, 1990), 47.

but quiet love, one that he knew, above all else, was irreplaceable. (*Five People,* 155–56)

My beloved is mine and I am his. (Song 2:16a)

As Albom notes, people speak of "finding" love as though it is hidden treasure or a long-forgotten trunk in the attic filled with valuables. Love is something we look for, something we search out. When we find it, make it, create it, we become possessive, often speaking in the language of ownership. We speak of those we love as belonging to us, most likely because we lack better terms. This sense of owning points to the wisdom that love is indeed specific. Beyond the chatter about soulmates lies the truth that our feelings of love are almost never general. They focus on one person. By so focusing, we experience a range of emotions in relationship to our particular person. Such is true for both the Shulammite and Eddie. For each of them love is indeed trained on one person. The connection is so focused and deep that it only takes the presence of the other to heighten and intensify emotions. This seems quite true for our Shulammite. Her descriptions of encounters with her love are filled with intense, physical responses that correspond to intense emotional responses. When the chorus of friends—the Daughters of Jerusalem—ask what the Shulammite finds so special about her shepherd, she offers six verses of poetry detailing his physical appearance (5:10–16), an appearance that she has already informed us makes her "faint with love" (5:8b). "I am my beloved's, / and his desire is for me" (7:10), she assures us, inviting her Shepherd out into the fields so that she may "give you my love" (7:12b). Clearly, the Shulammite believes her Shepherd to be the sole object of her love, and he returns that sense. He assures her that though Solomon may have had hundreds of women (vineyards), he has only one, and she "is for myself" (8:12).

She claims ownership over him in the same manner that a bulla marks ownership over a scroll among the scribes of ancient Israel. She declares that with powerful love comes powerful possessiveness. A woman who loves in this manner cannot share her man with other women. Such love is as strong as death; it utterly consumes the heart of the lover. She claims that such love is a rare, once-in-a-lifetime experience. Many never experience love at all. Like wisdom, it cannot be bought with money, and fidelity to one's bride is here equated with fidelity to Wisdom herself. Such a rare gift as love must be protected; to throw it away for a fling with an outsider would be the utmost folly.[8]

Although Albom does not present Eddie's love of Marguerite in terms quite so sensual, he does make much of Eddie's physical response to Marguerite. Their initial reunion finds Eddie reaching for her hand and feeling "as if flesh were forming over his own flesh, soft and warm and almost ticklish" (154). Completely overcome with feeling, Eddie finds himself sobbing on her shoulder. It is her, and her slightest touch causes "warmth [to] spread through his body" (156). Marguerite is Eddie's "only wife." The simple fact of her presence "ambush[ed] [Eddie] with old emotions, and his lips began to tremble and he was swept into the current of all that he had lost" with her death (159). Without cheapening the idea to a romantic cliché, Albom manages to point out to us the tendency we have of directing our most passionate love toward one person. This conclusion seems consistent with that of the Shulammite in Song. "The Song achieves something that medieval culture could not fathom and that modern and postmodern culture cannot artfully attain: a man and woman who maintain passionate desire for each other in the context of conventional morality."[9] Indeed, if both the Shulammite and Eddie realize that love only unfolds in one direction, they are among the wise.

---

[8]Garrett, 103.
[9]Ibid., 102.

Love Is Cyclical

Love, like rain, can nourish from above, drenching couples with a soaking joy. But sometimes, under the angry heat of life, love dries on the surface and must nourish from below, tending to its roots, keeping itself alive. (*Five People,* 164)

Upon my bed at night
  I sought him whom my soul loves;
I sought him, but found him not;
  I called him, but he gave no answer. (Song 3:1)

Love may be intense and singularly directed, but it also possesses a shadow side. Those who love wisdom know that love has a cycle of life that participates in growth, life, death, and renewal. Love is not always readily available nor does it always trumpet its appearance. Instead, it may go dormant, present but elusive. We will see this clearly in the experience of both sets of lovers.

Albom takes care to show us the shadow side of love, the times when hurts or betrayals cause partners to shut each other out.

While Song of Solomon does not speak about this explicitly, the Shulammite's dreams find her searching for a lover who has disappeared. Read metaphorically, the dark city through which she searches serves as a screen to hide her Shepherd physically, but also emotionally. Her lover is gone; she cannot find him anywhere. Even her search becomes a trial as the guards beat her for being out in the city after dark. (3:1–5; 5:2–8) Clearly, this love is not a constant presence, but instead quite elusive. We get an even better sense of this in chapter 5, where the Shulammite describes her lover's brief appearance at her door. He calls to her, but she waits a few beats too long. When she moves to let him in, he "had turned and was gone" (5:6). If her lover represents the concentrated passion of love, it seems telling that he comes and goes so quickly. Love's intensity, we might infer from this book, has a tendency to wax and wane.

While the Shulammite's circumstances appear more about the flames of passion than the slow burn of a constant love, Albom's portrait of Eddie and Marguerite deals with the nature of committed, long-term love. Recounting the lives of Eddie and Marguerite, Albom paints a romantic picture, not unlike that of the Shulammite and her Shepherd. They meet at the Stardust, dreamily dancing their way to love. She waits for him to return from war, not deterred by the darkness that accompanies him. Even their small financial resources, evidenced by the simple wedding in the Chinese restaurant, don't seem to damper the hopefulness of their future. We might spin all sorts of romantic tales of Marguerite and Eddie's life together.

Yet Albom also takes care to show us the shadow side of love, the times when hurts or betrayals cause them to shut each other out. Indeed, as we watch Eddie's depression worsen, his decisions cause a domino effect from which he cannot escape. Marguerite's accident while racing to the track proves instrumental here. They want to adopt a child. Preparing and waiting have fueled their love's intensity. But her injury and recovery cause them to miss out on the opportunity, and "the unspoken blame for this...moved like a shadow from husband to wife" (164).

Like the Shulammite, who does eventually find her Shepherd, Eddie and Marguerite recover, though Albom takes pains to emphasize the time it takes. "Their wound slowly healed," he writes, "and their companionship rose to fill the space they were saving for another" (165). Companionship is not passion, but it is the by-product of a bedrock love that may not always be intense, but is nonetheless secure.

Although we may acknowledge that each pair of lovers possesses a unique type of love, we can say with some degree of surety that both types display a cyclical nature. Lovers, no matter how intimate, do experience fallow times when they cannot seem to connect with their partner. Both Albom and Song's author portray this part of love with striking simplicity.

Love Has Multiple Forms

"Life has to end," she said. "Love doesn't."
(*Five People,* 173)

I adjure you, O daughters of Jerusalem,
> do not stir up or awaken love until it is ready!
(Song 8:4)

For the Shulammite, love's forms seem quite limited—love is passion, or it is pining. It never quite achieves a companionable balance or even a steady footing. Governed by spiteful brothers (8:8–9), she pursues her lover with extreme urgency. She clearly needs to be free of her family, and this heightens the intensity of her situation. "Don't interrupt us," she chides her friends. But she might just as well be warning them of love's fickle nature. "Don't pursue love so vigorously as I did," she warns. If she has learned anything from loving her Shepherd, and we as readers do indeed hope that she has, then perhaps she has learned to be more cautious, learned that passion does not last, that love comes to fruition in its own good time. Perhaps she has finally realized that love changes as lovers change and that perhaps that is why love can be so very good.

For Eddie and Marguerite, love does change and grow as they do. It begins exuberantly and passionately, mellows to a steady pleasure when he returns from war, and endures illness and disappointment throughout their time together. For them, love is more a verb than a noun. Love exists in the act of being together, in the act of doing. We see this best as their time together comes to a close. Eddie has spent all of this time in Marguerite's world—a feminine world made of endless wedding days and the joy surrounding them. His presence there indicates his strong desire to be a part of her, no matter where she is. He takes pleasure in telling her about forgiving his father, Albom indicates, feeling "an old, warm feeling he had missed for years, the simple act of making his wife happy" (170). Love, then, is a contented warmth. It is the panic induced by death. It is the extra glass of wine for the dying. It is also, as Marguerite insists, an act of remembrance. "I lost the only woman I ever loved," Eddie shouts. "No, you didn't," Marguerite replies. "I was right here. And you loved me anyway." Love is in the choosing, she implies, pointing out the purpose for the bridal dressing room.

Finally, what Eddie and Marguerite reveal to us is this: the act of loving evolves while the nature of love remains constant. "I don't want to go on. I want to stay here," Eddie murmurs while holding Marguerite. But she has already gone. Eddie finds himself alone again, perhaps experiencing another form of love: the bittersweet feelings of love rekindled and the disappointment of yet another loss.

The Shulammite also experiences loss. Indeed, the entire structure of Song leads to an unexpected conclusion. As Weems states it:

> In the first five chapters the lovers yearn for each other, delight in each other's charms, and sing each other's praises. In the last three chapters of the book, having defended their relationship against forces from without and from within, they eventually embrace, consummate their love, and pledge that their love, though costly, is more powerful than the forces opposing it. Under no circumstances can one argue that the book closes on a note of resolution or conclusion. At the end the maiden is forced to shoo her lover away, leaving the audience to wonder whether the two are ever allowed to relax and revel in their relationship. What could be the meaning of such an unresolved ending? Is love worth it? Perhaps that is precisely the question the song wants the audience to ponder.[10]

Love is specific. Love is cyclical. Love has multiple forms. Taken together, these three statements provide some of the

---

[10]Weems, *What Matters Most,* 373.

wisdom available to us through both Song and *The Five People*. Understanding some aspects of love's nature imparts the hope that someday we too may grasp the whole of what it means to love someone fully and to be loved in return.

QUESTIONS FOR DISCUSSION

1. What do you make of Albom's setting for this scene with Marguerite, Eddie's fourth visitor? Does it seem strange for Albom to reveal Eddie and Marguerite's story while they wander through others' weddings?
2. Since many commentators talk about Song of Solomon as an allegory for Jesus' love for the church, can you see any of the above wisdom about love as true of your church or community?
3. Some people believe that God chooses our mates, perhaps even creates specific people for us to love. Is this true for you? Do you think Albom believes this?
4. It is interesting that Eddie finally speaks of God in this section (171). What connections do you see between Eddie's joy at being with Marguerite and his curiosity about God?
5. Describe your own love in terms of being specific, cyclical, and possessing many forms. In what way(s) does your love not fit this pattern?
6. Is love a once-in-a-lifetime experience? Can love be both totally possessive and self-giving?
7. In your experience, is love worth it? Why? Why not?

FOR FURTHER READING

LaCocque, Andre. *Romance, She Wrote: A Hermeneutical Essay on Song of Songs*. Harrisburg, Pa.: Trinity Press International, 1998.

The New Interpreters Bible. Volume 5. Nashville: Abingdon Press, 1997.

Weems, Renita J. *What Matters Most: Ten Lessons in Living Passionately from the Song of Solomon*. West Bloomfield, Mich.: Warner Books with Walk Worthy Press, 2004.

CHAPTER FIVE

eddie and the voice from the whirlwind

"Why sad?" she said…Eddie sobbed…He said what he always said, to Marguerite, to Ruby, to the Captain, to the Blue Man, and more than anyone, to himself. "I was sad because I didn't do anything with my life. I was nothing. I accomplished nothing. I was lost. I felt like I wasn't supposed to be there."

(FIVE PEOPLE, 190–91)

"What is my strength, that I should wait?
*   And what is my end that I should be patient?*
Is my strength the strength of stones?
*   or is my flesh bronze?*
In truth I have no help in me,
*   and any resource is driven from me."*

(JOB 6:11–13)

Throughout his time in heaven, Eddie's search for wisdom, for the answer to the ultimate questions, presents him with various reasons for his life's course. Gathered nuggets of knowledge begin to create a whole picture for Eddie as he makes his way toward his final meeting. Finally, in the words of a child, Eddie finds the final puzzle piece that leads to his soul's peace. In this context we can look at Eddie via the story of another man also searching for the answer to the biggest questions ever—Job.

Job

It is presumptuous to comment on the book of Job. It is so full of the awesome reality of the living God. Like Job, one can only put one's hand over one's mouth (40:4)…The book of Job is about the unchanging human realities—war, destitution, sickness, humiliation, bereavement, depression. Also the unchanging goodness of God, who transforms our human agony into justice, kindness, love and joy. It is about "the terror of the Lord" (2 Cor. 5:11) and His great tenderness (Jas. 5:11). It is the story of one man who held on to his life in God with a faith that survived the torments of utter loss and expanded into new realms of wonder and delight.[1]

Joining the legion of presumptuous commentators, we need to understand basic information about the book of Job. Like many of the other texts classified as wisdom literature, the majority of Job's story is communicated in poetry, specifically in poetic dialogue, much as in the *Song of Solomon*. Job, too, has issues surrounding compositional dating and placement, though some scholars will place the final version in the late fifth or sixth century B.C.E.[2]

Moreover, scholars point out that although they cannot place the original tradition that the Job story emerged from, it has many parallels in Ancient Near Eastern lore. In particular, a text known as the *Babylonian Theodicy* presents striking parallels to the speeches of Job's friends. This lends credence to the idea that Near Eastern wisdom thinkers created a tradition of wisdom dialogues concerning the nature and justice of suffering.

When biblical scholars study a text, they can often identify where layers of the story have been added or changed by scribes at various times in history. The book of Job is no different. Relying on the theory that many of the Old Testament stories arise from an ancient oral storytelling tradition, Job scholars point to the structure of Job as evidence that it derives from

---

[1] Francis I. Andersen, *Job*, Tyndale Old Testament Commentaries (Leicester: InterVarsity Press, 1976), 9.

[2] The abbreviation B.C.E. stands for "before common era," a designation that means the text came about prior to the beginning of the common era (C.E. or what used to be referred to as A.D., "After Death," meaning after the death of Jesus). David J. A. Clines, *Job 1–20*, Word Biblical Commentary, vol. 17 (Dallas: Word Books, 1989), lvii, spreads the dating to "some point between the seventh and the second centuries....the author has succeeded well in disguising his own age and background in his creation of the character of his hero."

more than one source. Indeed, Job 1:1—2:13 appears as a prose story about a man who patiently accepts his suffering, refusing to speak ill of the God who causes it. In contrast, the poetic dialogues encased in 3:1 through 42:6 present a Job intent on forcing God to articulate God's reasoning for afflicting one so upstanding as himself. Here Job debates with three friends in three cycles:

FRIEND	CYCLE ONE	CYCLE TWO	CYCLE THREE
Eliphaz	chapters 4—5	15	22
Job	6—7	16—17	23—24
Bildad	8	18	25
Job	9—10	19	26
Zophar	11	20	?
Job	12—14	21	27

Job's apparent closing statement (28—31) finds unexpected response from an interloper on the scene—Elihu—in chapters 32—37. Then God takes center stage for a conversation with Job (38:1—42:6). The tale's end (42:7–12) then reverts to prose and presents a rather awkward finale that many scholars think contains the seeds of the original folktale. David Clines has argued for the original unity of the book on literary grounds. He concedes that Job is a patient sufferer in the prose introduction but a vehement accuser of God in the poetry. God's personal name Yahweh appears in prose, not in poetry. Also, the prose details the cause of Job's troubles, but this cause appears to be unknown in the dialogues. For Clines, Job's change is dramatically satisfying. God's name is not used, because the friends are not presented as worshipers of Yahweh. The cause of suffering is unknown, because it is a transaction in heaven not revealed on earth. The prose and poetry are structurally joined. The friends' arrival in chapter 2 prepares for their dialogues with Job. The address to the friends in the closing prose section (42:7–8) presupposes the friends' opposition to

Job in the poetry. The prose narrative is not complete without something intervening between its two parts, something very much like the poetic speeches. The story of Job may be much older than the book, but in the present form "the author of the prologue and the epilogue is also the poet of the dialogues and wrote the prose framework deliberately for its present place in the book."[3]

Scholars vary widely in their interpretations of Job beyond structure. Indeed, the sorts of questions that emerge from this text occupy a broad spectrum and can deal with any number of issues. Perhaps the most prominent is the question of the proper response to suffering. Is it, as Job's friends suggest, acceptance and then repentance? Is suffering truly something handed out on the basis of one's sins? These sorts of questions are part and parcel of any exploration of theodicy—the nature of evil. Is evil inherent in the world? Is God the author of evil? This line of thought, of course, leads to broader theological issues surrounding the nature of God. Is God always just? Does God wield retributive powers, and, if so, is that ultimately fair? In short, just what kind of God does Job worship and, by association, what sort of God do we, the faithful readers, worship?

These are indeed deep questions that may have as many answers as readers. While some might read Job's final concession to God as an act of contrition, others have argued that throughout the piece, Job parodies language found in various psalms and hymns, and therefore is only humoring the deity. Moreover, Job's story ends with God's proclaiming Job's righteousness and scolding his friends who insisted on his sinfulness. However, the friends were not entirely wrong; God did indeed return Job's family, home, and possessions. The story-world of Job then, is one that is ultimately unpredictable and vastly open to interpretation. And in interpretation lies the

---

[3]Clines, lviii.

key to our own exploration of Job as it relates to Eddie's final conversation in heaven.

Job and Eddie

As we noted before, Job is a complicated text. This fact makes our work harder as we seek to put these two stories into conversation. To begin with, we can note such wide differences not only in time and place but also in the level of devastation. While Job loses all he has ever had—his home, his family, his livelihood—Eddie's despair is a product of unrealized dreams. In this way, Job's situation seems much more intense than Eddie's does. Of course, the similarities are glaringly obvious—both Eddie and Job are searching for an answer as they ask WHY?

To begin this dialogue, we need to make one crucial distinction about the questions Eddie and Job ask. Job does not ask what the purpose of his life is, or even really about the purpose of his suffering. Rather, Job poses a question outside of himself. That is, Job wants to know the nature of *God's* purpose. By contrast, Eddie looks solely at himself. He does not seem to wonder about the nature of God or about God's reasons for denying his dreams. In fact, he doesn't really seem to be aware of God as a powerful presence at all. Instead, he seems to want to know what his own purpose was and why he ended up "stuck" at Ruby Pier.

This difference fuels our discussion of the two texts, because from this we can address two contingent issues: (1) What does each character understand to be the power inherent in his world? (2) What is this power like? By looking closely at these questions, we hope to be able to come to some sort of conclusion about the wisdom available in these texts.

Fate or Providence

[Eddie] felt as if he'd tumbled down steps and was crumpled at the bottom. His soul was vacant. He had no impulse. (*Five People,* 179)

"Oh, that I knew where I might find him,
    that I might come even to his dwelling!
I would lay my case before him,
    and fill my mouth with arguments.
I would learn what he would answer me,
    and understand what he would say to me."
(Job 23:3–5)

The key to understanding both Job and Eddie is to take a good look at how they envision "the other." By "other" I mean that which exerts power over them. In our consideration of Eddie, this comes not just from looking at the episode involving the fifth person he meets, but also from our collected sense of Eddie. We can begin by noting that throughout his time in heaven Eddie does not determine his own path. Rather, we get the sense that he moves from scene to scene in a predetermined way over which he cannot exert any influence. He does not choose whom he meets. Instead they choose him. Eddie then becomes a passive agent, hanging "limp and lifeless in the void, as if on a hook, as if all the fluids had been gored out of him" (180). He wants to spend more time with Marguerite but knows that "there was no way to reach or call or wave or even look at her picture" (179). Eddie does not even have control over when he moves to the next person. Instead he must wait in total ignorance until a "small but haunting noise" awakens him. Even then he responds by clutching his fist, a "lifelong defense instinct" (180). Clearly, Eddie's demeanor signals the disconnect between himself and whatever entity is running the show.

From our total knowledge of Eddie, we understand this to be true of his life as well. While he dreams of becoming an engineer, he takes relatively few steps to accomplish that dream. His return from war with a "bum leg" seems to seal the deal. He returns to work at Ruby Pier, moving into the apartment he grew up in. Indeed, Eddie's profound disillusionment throughout his life speaks to his sense of helplessness. Although

Marguerite is a fighter and seems to tackle life head-on, Eddie just lets things happen. He then seals the hurt, disappointment, or anger inside, failing to vent any of it.

From our time with Eddie we can begin to conclude that he simply does not understand God as an active force in his life. He doesn't speak of God, or anything at all religious for that matter. Rather, his attitudes reveal a man resigned to fate, a man who perceives life as a cruel joke perpetuated by some unfeeling other, over which he has no control. Fate, or even life itself, only gives Eddie a hard time.

Unlike Eddie's impersonal sense of fate, Job's understanding of God is very personal. For Job, God is not an old man in the sky, but instead an immanent presence. We can see this immediately, given that Job actually names God, while Eddie never has any sense of fate or God, only blaming life's disappointments on his own lameness. So Job has a specific deity to whom he relates in a personal way by offering sacrifices and prayers. Moreover, Job has a working knowledge of God's power: "that it would please God to crush me," Job tells his friends in 6:9, "that he would let loose his hand and cut me off!" (6:9). Clearly, Job's God has power over life and death, assigning illness and destruction at will. However, this does not discourage Job. Although his friends continue to counsel him to simply confess his sins and repent, Job refuses to do so. God does not work that way, he insists, arguing, "[God] destroys both the blameless and the wicked" (9:22*b*). God, it seems, is in charge, is larger than life, and is completely capricious in handing out terror. "The God of the friends is so domesticated, so restrained, so predictable. Job knows of no such God. His raw experience has taught him otherwise. When Job speaks of God, awe and terror are in his words."[4]

We might think that because Job understands God's ultimate power, Job himself would simply sit in abject misery

---

[4]John C. Holbert, *Preaching Job* (St. Louis: Chalice Press, 1999), 158.

awaiting God's reversal of his fortunes. Indeed, this might be the Job of the original folktale, but not the Job we know in the received text. Maintaining his innocence, Job becomes his own best advocate, informing his friends, "I have understanding as well as you…I, who called upon God and he answered me. / a just and blameless man, I am a laughingstock" (12:3a, 4). Here we see again that the God Job knows intimately has betrayed him. Therefore, Job feels justified in calling God out, demanding that God appear and defend the horrors inflicted Job.

John Holbert reminds readers and preachers of Job's integrity:

> Do not hear his words only as the ravings of an arrogant man, one who needs a great infusion of humility if he is to come before his God. Job is ready to come before the mysterious God precisely because he refuses to play the theological games of the friends. Job will never admit in any way that they are right. But note, too, that he will never speak injustice or utter deceit. By that he means he will call a spade a spade, let the chips fall where they may. His raw experience is true for him; he will not disguise it, sweeten it, nuance it, or in any way deny it. Job comes to God as Job, not some approximation of Job, not some Job as he wishes he were, certainly not the Job the friends wanted him to be. The word often used for such a person is integrity.[5]

In other words, while Eddie looks to understand himself, Job looks to understand God in an increasingly aggressive, but honest, subpoena.

Suffering Is a Part of Life?

"The *nipa*. Ina say be safe there. Wait for her. Be safe. Then big noise. Big fire. You burn me." She shrugged her narrow shoulders. "Not safe." (*Five People,* 188)

---

[5]Ibid., 161–62.

"Therefore I have uttered what I did not understand,
   things too wonderful for me, which I did not know.
'Hear and I will speak;
   I will question you, and you declare to me.'
I had heard of you by the hearing of the ear,
   but now my eye sees you;
therefore I despise myself,
   and repent in dust and ashes." (Job 42:3b-6)

If Eddie's search is for himself, for the reasons fate kept him from his dreams, then perhaps his meeting with Tala produces the most vivid picture of the paradox in which he finds himself. A man who never had children, a man who is, like Job, blameless in his own eyes, confronts his worst deed in a pidgin conversation with a small child. "You burn me," she says (187); and Eddie, having just finished one of his pipe cleaner sculptures, transforms in our minds from a kind, albeit pathetic, figure to a child-killer.

"The darkness that had shadowed him all those years was revealing itself at last, it was real, flesh and blood, this child, this lovely child, he had killed her, burned her to death" (188), Albom tells us. Harmless, passive Eddie, whose life was governed by an inflexible Fate, must come to grips with the enormity of his actions. "He wailed then...until the howling gave way to prayerlike utterances," (188–89) and his words became those of confession: "I killed you, I KILLED YOU," then a whispered "forgive me," then, "FORGIVE ME, OH GOD...What have I done...WHAT HAVE I DONE?" (189).

Clearly Eddie sees himself for the first time as an active participant in the drama that was his life. In a life full of blame and avoidance, Eddie comes only in his death to understand himself as an actor. He comes face-to-face with a mistake that had fatal consequences for a child, a mistake he had made unknowingly. His intentions were not to murder Tala, and yet that is what he had done. His choice of active verbs reveals the ownership he claims. We can hardly escape the irony of it, and yet Albom does not leave the cruel joke hanging in the air. Instead, Tala hands Eddie a rock.

"You wash me," she says, transforming from beautiful child to repulsive burn victim. Eddie takes the stone and, like Tala's *ina* or mother, he steps into the river and begins to rub her skin as if cleansing her for a special event. We should not miss the significance here. Water, long a symbol of forgiveness and redemption, signals the onset of Eddie's release, and his rubbing action with the stone returns Tala to her true self, the scabs and scars falling away. Tala, Eddie's conduit to heaven, turns out to be his savior. She not only guides him on his journey, she emerges as the only person able to confront Eddie with himself and provide him with grace. She replaces Fate and his impersonal other. In some sense this small child emerges as his God-figure. In this role she alone has the answer to the haunting question: Did he save the little girl at Ruby Pier? "You keep her safe," Tala says (192), and the river current carries Eddie away as though it were the current of his own relief.

If Eddie finally encounters himself in a revelation that transforms him from passive receiver of life to active participant, can we say the same for Job? Is there anything in Job's story that might indicate a shift in thought or understanding? Here it seems appropriate to point to Job's responses to God's monologues. God's appearance furthers our picture of God's relationship with Job as personal. Indeed, Job calls, and God eventually shows up. Unlike Eddie, Job knows himself, believes himself an innocent victim of God's criminal acts. But God's appearance does not ensure the reckoning Job was counting on. Instead of offering a courtroom-worthy defense, God throws down a glove. "Gird up your loins like a man, / I will question you, and you shall declare to me" (38:3). In other words, God has no intention of defending God's actions, but instead intends to put Job on the defensive by challenging his understanding.

"Where were you when I laid the foundation of the earth?" God asks (38:4*a*). As God continues in this fashion, it becomes clear that God finds Job's demands just a bit much. Recounting God's own creative acts, God initially appears to support Job's friends' position—God can and will do as God sees fit, rewarding and punishing as God chooses. However, God is quite a bit more subtle than that. Notice that although God grandstands about the vastness of creation, God refrains from directly addressing Job's accusations. By doing so, God demonstrates the power God holds.

God is so powerful God does not even have to answer Job's charges. In this way, Job fades from angry warrior demanding justice into a subdued man who, whether he means it or not, voices the very repentance he swore to withhold: "Therefore I despise myself, / and repent in dust and ashes" (42:6). Ultimately Job, like Eddie, discovers his place in the world. He is no longer an aggressive challenger choosing his path, but instead a mere human admitting that "I know that you [God] can do all things, / and that no purpose of yours can be thwarted" (42:2).

But does this change in Job's perspective mean that the book of Job has nothing to say about human suffering? Obviously the book was not written to explain suffering and does not give an explicit defense of God. It does show us perspectives on the issue that we must consider carefully. James Crenshaw lists eight understandings of suffering in the book of Job, and "all of these understandings of suffering in one way or another find expression in the book of Job."

1. Retributive grounded in the order of the universe and the will of the creator;
2. Disciplinary grounded in family life and the loving punishment of children;
3. Probative grounded in God's testing of people to see if religion is pure, having replaced self-interest with the centrality of holiness;
4. Eschatological grounded in hope in God for the future that makes present suffering insignificant;

5. Redemptive grounded in the sacrificial system's provision of atonement;
6. Revelatory grounded in God's revelation of human pride and divine mystery through suffering;
7. Ineffable grounded in divine mystery about which humans cannot speak and before which humans cannot demand knowledge;
8. Incidental grounded in the understanding of a God who placed suffering in the creation as part of the human condition.[6]

Still, with all these responses to suffering, we must remember that "for Job, God has no right to cause suffering to come upon a person unless that person deserves punishment. The proper response where suffering appears to be undeserved is not humble prayer but confrontation of God. Thus Job rejects the notion of unconditional piety, at least insofar as it would mean submission to a God who acts without regard to what is just."[7]

Notions of Justice

Finally then, what wisdom can we discern by looking at the transformations these two characters undergo? I want to suggest to you that we are not looking for wisdom about suffering, or about the purpose of life, or even about the nature of God. Rather, what comes through both these texts are notions of justice, tiny glimmers of what it might mean to be human in a world God created.

For Eddie the idea of justice might, on first glance, appear to have much to do with what one deserves. He killed a child. Granted he did so unknowingly, but the girl died nonetheless. Eddie's dream, then, must have been denied because he committed

[6]James L. Crenshaw, "Job, Book of," in *Anchor Bible Dictionary,* vol. 3 (New York: Doubleday, 19??), 865–66.
[7]Carol A. Newsom, "The Book of Job," in *New Interpreter's Bible,* vol. 4 (Nashville: Abingdon Press, 1996), 334–35.

an unforgivable sin. This is, of course, the position Job's friends take. God punishes the wicked and rewards the faithful. In their view, Job, subjected to such thorough devastation, must have committed a particularly egregious act. Repentance is the cure, and restoration of fortunes is God's intent.

Yet God does not side with the friends, instead instructing them to "offer up for yourselves a burnt offering; and my servant Job shall pray for you" (42:8). Job, declares God, has "spoken of me what is right" (42:8). Then, in an even more enigmatic move, God restores all Job's fortunes twice over. Clearly then, neither Job nor his friends are completely right about God. They have spun theology to the very edge of their wits, but have not fully grasped the nature of the divine. This, it seems finally, is the paradox of God—you must continually search for understanding, relying on God's justice, even as you admit that the ways of God are much too mysterious to grasp. In this context, then, justice becomes the opportunity to pursue God, to live in God's world complete with the Behemoth (40:15) and the Leviathan (41:1)—metaphors for the dark and terrifying that must exist in God's world so that we, in some way, can embrace the good.

So what about Eddie? What sort of justice does he get? What wisdom can we find here? We can, I think, tease out the beginning of an answer by looking briefly at a short scene with Eddie and Tala. Here we encounter the fullness of Tala's revelation: "'Ina say be safe there. Wait for her. Be safe. Then big noise. Big fire. You burn me.' She shrugged her narrow shoulders. 'Not safe'" (188).

Notice here that Tala's tone is not angry or demanding, but rather matter-of-fact. Her mother thought the barn was safe, but it wasn't. That's how life goes, she seems to say with the shoulder shrug. Yes, Eddie caused the fire, but her death wasn't anyone's fault per se; who knew that the barn wouldn't be safe? Moreover, even as Eddie weeps for himself, for the destruction he caused, she doesn't tell him he should be crying; nor does she reassure him. Rather, she sits there playing with her pipe cleaner dog next to the idyllic riverbank, a nonjudgmental presence in Eddie's grief.

We could easily argue that the grief he suffers over knowing his part in Tala's death was Eddie's proper justice, but again the issue seems much more complicated. Eddie's justice is patently unlike Job's in that Eddie does not get his life back. He does not get to relive the war, to choose not to blow up the barn, to choose to overcome his depression and lameness. Instead, Eddie gets wisdom. He finds a fullness denied to Job, because Tala reveals to him the effects of his life. By working at Ruby Pier and keeping rides safe, Eddie kept thousands of children safe from harm, kept them alive and enjoying life. "Children," Tala says, "You keep them safe. You make good for me" (191).

While we could posit that Eddie's life course was his punishment for Tala's death, we might be better off realizing that a pier full of safe children was not punishment. Rather, the children represented the outcome of a life lived faithfully—a life in which one comes to work every day, does one's job well, and learns to take a measure of satisfaction in that. Eddie finds this satisfaction in heaven instead of in life, but he does find it. And that seems to be the purpose to the whole tale.

So we see that while Job and Eddie possess similar elements and even follow similar patterns, ultimately they come up on different ends of the spectrum. In both tales knowledge, and by extension wisdom, exists as the object of justice. Yet the tales do not agree on the nature of wisdom. For Job, only God possesses wisdom. Human beings can strive to achieve a level of understanding, but they cannot ever fathom God's wisdom in its entirety. The book of Job, then, exists as a piece of theology, a work whose express purpose is to expose and examine God.

Albom's message is infinitely different. He does not deal with the person or nature of God. By thinking about ontology (being) instead of theology (nature of God), Albom presents a world where wisdom, defined as full knowledge of one's self and world, is the ultimate reward.

QUESTIONS FOR FURTHER DISCUSSION

1. Before thinking about the story of Job in this context, what were your impressions of it? What message did you believe it was sending and why?

2. Do you believe that God rewards the faithful and punishes the wicked? Do you imagine God's grace as abundant or scarce? Why?

3. What sorts of injustices do you see in the world, and what do you believe to be God's role in those?

4. Which picture of justice do you find yourself agreeing with? Do you hope for full understanding of yourself as a part of the afterlife, or do you believe that only God will ever completely understand? Why? In what ways would you nuance these categories?

5. Do you see yourself as Eddie, a passive entity acted upon, or as Job, an active participant demanding an accounting from God?

6. How do you begin to answer the question of why innocent people suffer undeservedly? Are any of the eight answers provided by James Crenshaw satisfying for you? Why? Why not?

7. Can there truly be an answer to life's injustice apart from God?

8. What motivates you to continue living and striving to accomplish when you do not understand the troubles and unanswerable questions that plague your life?

9. Would Eddie have lived differently if he had had the answers from the five people he met before he died?

FOR FURTHER READING

Dell, Katharine. *Shaking a Fist at God: Struggling with the Mystery of Undeserved Suffering.* Ligouri, Mo.: Triumph Books, 1995.

The New Interpreter's Bible. Volume 4. Nashville: Abingdon Press, 1997.

Perdue, Leo G., and W. Clark Gilpin, eds. *The Voice from the Whirlwind: Interpreting the Book of Job.* Nashville: Abingdon Press, 1992.

CHAPTER SIX

where eddie and wisdom beckon

*And in that line now was a whiskered old man,
with a linen cap and a crooked nose, who waited in
a place called the Stardust Band Shell to share his
part of the secret of heaven: that each affects the other
and the other affects the next, and the world is full of
stories, but the stories are all one.*

(*Five People*, 196)

*[Wisdom] calls from the highest places in the town,
"You that are simple, turn in here!"
    To those without sense she says,
"Come, eat of my bread
    and drink of the wine I have mixed.
Lay aside immaturity, and live,
    and walk in the way of insight."*

(Prov. 9:3–6)

For the first five chapters of our book, we have viewed the five people Eddie met through lenses forged out of the wisdom texts of the Hebrew Bible. Now, as *Five People* ends, we find ourselves at the end of Eddie's journey to heaven. He has met five different people, all of whom have been waiting for him in order to explain and further nuance the meaning of his life. Now it is Eddie's time to wait. One day the little girl whose life he saved on the day he died will come to his heaven on the way to her own, and they will get the chance to meet.

She will discover that Eddie has joined the vast web of eternity to which the Blue Man, Marguerite, the Captain, Ruby, and Tala belong. Eddie will then have the privilege of sharing with her some insights into the meaning of her life.

It might seem that by now we must have exhausted the parallels between Eddie's journey and the wisdom traditions. While there might be some truth to such a thought, it is also just as true that we still have room to examine what the wisdom traditions and *Five People* may ultimately tell us about our own lives.

Wisdom and the Information Age

Spawned by continuous technological growth, a globally dominant economy, and sophisticated and ubiquitous mass communication systems, North Americans live in a culture deluged by information. This flood of information has given individuals a vast array of choices, whether those choices concern educational opportunities, career paths, or consumer goods. However, having this amount of information can lead to lives that are intensely complicated. In a recent article in *The Atlantic Monthly,* Ian Frazier mused over the complications of living in the "information age":

> If despair is a sin (and it is—it's an aspect of the deadly sin of sloth), the virtuous person must resist it, and all tendencies likely to lead to it. Torturing the mind with minutiae is one of those…Look down the table at the public library where people plug in their laptops, and see the heaped-up entanglement of cables and wires. Try to read the pamphlet in six-point type that your new phone carrier sends you when you change long-distance service. Go to the supermarket to buy an ordinary item for your spouse. The other day at the A&P I noticed a man lost in thought in front of a bank of different kinds of brownie mix. Then he took out his cell phone and made a call: "Hi, babe…You wanted Triple Chunk? Okay…I thought you said Triple *Fudge* Chunk." At some point the brain, in order to avoid despair, begins to shut down.[1]

A life filled purely with information can be, as Frazier suggests, emotionally crippling. Perhaps that explains the success of a book such as *The Five People You Meet in Heaven,* which is

---

[1] Ian Frazier, "If Memory Doesn't Serve," *The Atlantic Monthly* (October 2004): 107.

a parable about the meaning of life. It deals with questions that cannot be answered by installing and learning the intricacies of new software or by researching statistics on the Web site of a cable news network. Perhaps *Five People* has given readers a chance to depart (if only momentarily) from answering questions, providing solutions, and making plans based on concrete, empirical information. Instead *Five People* has allowed them to engage in questions that are spiritual in nature: *What happens to me after I die?*—or perhaps more important—*What does my life* **mean***?*

These are questions that are worth asking, but they are questions that we do not always think we have the chance to ask. Even in many religious communities, questions about capital campaigns or curriculum choices, personnel concerns or maintenance issues prove so exhausting that they leave little opportunity to explore in much detail questions about existence and what life is all about. However, they are questions that we all ask—even if we only get around to asking them after a long day at work, after kids' extracurricular activities, after studying for work or school, after answering e-mails, or after programming the new TiVo system. In this way, *Five People*— like Ecclesiastes, Job, and the other wisdom literature—invites us to consider the possibilities of what we're doing with our time and how the seemingly mundane things we have to do might impact the lives of strangers.

Wisdom and the God We Seek

As we have mentioned several times throughout this book, wisdom literature exhibits a theology of a much different character than much of the Hebrew Bible. The covenant between Israel and YHWH, for example, is not an explicit part of the theology of Proverbs. Ecclesiastes, for example, expresses a fatalism absent from the rest of the Hebrew Bible.

Recently many scholars have examined the character of Lady Wisdom (Sophia or *Hokmah*), the personification of wisdom found in Proverbs 9 (a portion of which opens this chapter). Some have suggested that Lady Wisdom may be a remnant of an ancient Israelite goddess tradition, suppressed by those favoring the YHWHist tradition. Of course, many see monotheism not as a historical or anthropological development, but as an absolute truth rooted in the existence of a personal God whose existence is not conceived by human beings, but revealed through God's action in history. For these people this notion threatens long-held assumptions about the beliefs and practices of the ancient Israelites. The recent insights have made the wisdom traditions seem subversive—and dangerous—to some religious communities. However, in a recent edition of *The Biblical Preaching Journal,* Michael Williams suggests that it is not the possibility of an embedded goddess in the wisdom traditions that makes them problematic for religious communities to deal with:

> The danger of wisdom material is not, as some suggested during the Sophia controversy, that we will all end up dancing hand-in-hand with lady wisdom around a graven image around some goddess. Rather, wisdom's harmful influence is much more subtle and insidious; that is to convince us that the mysteries of life and faith are finally reducible to ethical formulas. Wisdom runs the risk of leaving us with the impression that the radically free YHWH of biblical narrative is really a very predictable and manageable elderly relative who just wants us to be "good little children." The problem is that we wind up worshipping human virtue rather than the God of biblical tradition.[2]

Williams makes an excellent point. The ambiguities of life, the complexities of what it means to live ethically, and the utter mystery of the universe and the God whom we worship make it impossible to believe that the admonitions of Proverbs

---

[2]Michael Williams, "Exegesis for 'The Wise and Compassionate Judge,'" *Biblical Preaching Journal,* 17, no. 4 :10.

sum up what it means to live a life of faith. However, our examination of the whole collection of wisdom literature has revealed that the tradition offers us much more than a simplistic cause-and-effect theology. These texts express a fair diversity of approaches, styles, and genres. All seek to answer questions about the meaning of life in a variety of nuanced ways. Whereas the scribes who authored Proverbs focus on how to order life in a "wise," conventional way, the writer(s) of Ecclesiastes delves into a pragmatism that allows for a sense of radical existential doubt.

Interestingly enough, when we put the wisdom traditions and *Five People* side-by-side, we discover a theme running through both collections—our actions have consequences. Proverbs and the wisdom psalms, of course, examine this theme with a type of moral certainty. They say that your actions, whether foolish or wise, have consequences, so choose wise and virtuous actions in order to reap livable results. Ecclesiastes and Job, however, take a different perspective. Often offering ideas that serve as a critique of the clear-cut logic of Proverbs, these books explore suffering as a mystery that ultimately only God can answer.

Five People, likewise, emphasizes that our actions have consequences, even if these consequences are often unknown to us and completely unintended. Nonetheless, the things we do often put events into play that affect others in profound ways. While *Five People* does not weave this thought into a system of moral instruction such as the one in Proverbs, it does leave readers with a sense of the nature of God that is very similar to one aspect shared by most of the wisdom literature we have examined: Even if life seems vain, even if suffering is unjust, ultimately God redeems injustice, pointlessness, and suffering. Even Ecclesiastes and Job end with the admission of God's sovereignty. In *Five People,* Eddie's journey culminates in a beautiful invitation to Eddie from God—a single word that simultaneously welcomes, redeems, forgives, and validates Eddie's life: "*Home.*"

Ultimately, wisdom literature and Albom's parable leave us with a sense of a God who cares for humanity, but who gives us autonomy and free will. Of course, having the ability to make our own decisions and interpret the world as we see it certainly has consequences—sometimes life will seem vain, suffering will rarely seem just, and we will not always see the presence of God. However, at its best, wisdom literature reminds us that the presence of God is as mysterious as the question of suffering, and that, just as Albom reminds us, it may take longer than a lifetime to discover the answers to our whys.

Eddie and Lady Wisdom

The mysterious Lady Wisdom of the Bible serves as an interesting figure for readers of wisdom literature. In the text, she stands in the street, inviting all those who will hear to enter into a new way of living—she promises understanding that will lead to spiritual fulfillment. She provides us, as readers, an entrance into a part of the biblical tradition that many of us have left unexamined, and thereby invites us into new ways of looking at the nature of God.

Eddie serves the readers of *Five People* in a very similar way. Not only will he provide insight to the young girl for whom he waits, but he has been our guide, as we have watched his life unfold in Albom's parable, giving us insight, and giving voice to many of the questions and uncertainties we have. His questions about the meaning of life have been our questions, and his journey has exemplified the journey toward understanding on which we all hope to embark. Although we may never know the absolute, definitive answers that Eddie and the others in Albom's novel have received, thanks to Eddie we have been privy to a story that mirrors our own hopes and dreams and leaves us just a bit wiser than we were before we perused its pages.

QUESTIONS FOR DISCUSSION

1. What do you think about the perspective of the wisdom traditions? Does it seem to complement ideas about God found in other parts of the Bible?
2. What do you see as the differences between knowledge, information, and wisdom?
3. What do you see as similarities between the wisdom traditions and *The Five People You Meet in Heaven*?
4. How do the wisdom traditions and *The Five People You Meet in Heaven* reflect your own dreams? your own doubts?
5. How has reading this guide affected your understanding and beliefs about heaven? about life on earth?

FOR FURTHER READING

Frazier, Ian. "If Memory Doesn't Serve." *The Atlantic Monthly.* October 2004.

Williams, Michael. "Exegesis for 'The Wise and Compassionate Judge,'" *Biblical Preaching Journal* 17, no. 4: 10.

POPULAR INSIGHTS

In the Popular Insights series, widely read books are an entry into theological discussions, Bible and church history, scripture, and new understandings of ourselves and how we live in community. For individual readers and discussion groups.

UNVEILING THE SECRET LIFE OF BEES
by Amy Lignitz Harken

In conversation with the Bible and Sue Monk Kidd's best-selling novel *The Secret Life of Bees* (Penguin Books, 2003), *Unveiling the Secret Life of Bees* explores the embodiments of women, feminine power, relationships, and the importance of women in the life of the church. It looks at the roles of women in the Bible and how those roles are defined or redefined in *The Secret Life of Bees,* expanding our concepts of "holy mother," earthly mothers, sisters, daughters, wives, and "queen bee." Along the way, we encounter remembrance, forgiveness, reconciliation, liberation, community, rituals, the feminine face of God, and the important role women play in one another's lives.

• 0-8272-3026-5, $12.99

SOLVING THE DA VINCI CODE MYSTERY
by Brandon Gilvin

Drawing on the Bible, non-canonical texts, and a wealth of historical thought and contemporary scholarship, *Solving the Da Vinci Code Mystery* helps readers to separate fact from fiction in Dan Brown's *The Da Vinci Code* (Doubleday, 2003). Rather than just discrediting or debunking the theories posed in *The Da Vinci Code, Solving the Da Vinci Code Mystery* uses Dan Brown's postulates to explore the importance of the issues raised in the novel.

• 0-8272-3457-0, $12.99

CHALICE 1-800-366-3383 • www.chalicepress.com
PRESS